Water Polo Whiz

Water Polo Whiz

Chuck Hines

authorHOUSE®

AuthorHouse™
1663 Liberty Drive
Bloomington, IN 47403
www.authorhouse.com
Phone: 1-800-839-8640

Photographer Don Jedlovec

Published by AuthorHouse 10/07/2014

ISBN: 978-1-4969-4331-6 (sc)
ISBN: 978-1-4969-4330-9 (e)

INTRODUCTION

By Chuck Hines

This is a fictional novel that takes place in the present, but it's based on my 55-year involvement with the Olympic sport of water polo, especially the time I spent teaching and coaching at the Asheville YMCA in Western North Carolina. Before coming to Asheville in 1969, I worked for Ys in Minneapolis-St. Paul, Minnesota, and Des Moines, Iowa, and Canton, Illinois, and I was a water polo player and coach at each of these communities. For historical information about the sport and my participation, I refer you to a prior book that I wrote, *Water Polo the Y's Way,* available from AuthorHouse and other sources.

I was aided in writing and publishing these two books by members of the Asheville YMCA Water Polo Alumni Club. These are players whom I coached during the 1970s and 1980s. They now range in age from 45 to 60 and reside in cities across the country. Some have continued to play water polo at the Masters level. In recent years, we've communicated regularly via email and have enjoyed frequent lunch gatherings in Asheville, to which many of these former players have returned from as far away as Florida, Maine, Colorado, and California.

I am indebted to these men and women. As young teens, they enabled me to look good as a coach when our Asheville teams won 10 national AAU and YMCA tournaments and represented the U.S. internationally. Nowadays they remain supportive of my efforts by contributing financially and literally to the writing that I do. All of us – they as players and I as the coach – benefited from their parents, some still living but others having departed for the Afterlife. It's the parents who make it all possible, both in the factual past and in this fictional novel.

Thus before starting to tell the tale of the *Water Polo Whiz*, I feel the need to take time and acknowledge the players from the past, my past, who deserve recognition. They played on our various YMCA teams. We fielded three different boys' teams and four different girls' teams from 1970 through 1980, so you might become a bit confused in trying to discern who played for which team, and exactly when. Be that as it may, here, in some semblance of alphabetical order, is a list of 40 of Asheville's top aces from the past.

Barbara and Libby Anderson – *These sisters played on our girls' team that earned the silver medal at the 1975 Junior Olympics. Barbara, a swift swimmer, was a 1975 Honorable Mention Junior All-American. Libby, the younger one and a stalwart defender, came back two years later to compete in the 1977 Junior Olympics and, like her sister, was an Honorable Mention Junior All-American.*

Molly (Griffin) Bachmann – *What's the secret to success? Hard work. Molly demonstrated this vital characteristic during her water polo days. A slow swimmer at the start, she put in the hours necessary to reach the top, earning Junior All-America honors in 1972 and Senior All-America status in 1975. She was MVP at the 1976 Women's Junior Nationals and concluded her competitive career by participating in the 1977 World Women's Club Championships.*

Rob Baker – *He was my right-hand man in the Asheville YMCA water polo program for many years. He played on our boys' team that won the 1973 Y Nationals, receiving all-tournament recognition. He kept on playing Masters water polo in the 1980s and 1990s and was still playing as recently as 2009-2010. He also served as one of my assistant coaches. Along the way, Rob was selected as a YMCA All-American.*

Mary Alice (Stickney) Bell – *She was one of the players on our initial girls' team in 1969-1970 and played in the 1970 and 1971 Junior Olympics and on our winning teams at the 1971 Women's Junior Nationals and 1972 YMCA Nationals. The Stickney family has been one of the Asheville YMCA's leading supporters for 50 or more years.*

Diana (Wieder) Braun – *Like her close friend, Mary Alice Bell, Diana was one of our original players who competed in the aforementioned 1970, 1971, and 1972 national tournaments. She was an Honorable Mention Junior All-American. Then her family moved to another state. Recently, Diana returned to North Carolina, and she's a member of our Alumni Club.*

Phil Cocke – *Moving from the YMCA's basketball court to the pool as a young teen, he was a standout poloist from the moment he began playing. He received the MVP Award at the 1973 Y Nationals, which our Asheville boys won. He was a Prep All-American. His highest-scoring game was 10 goals. Phil was a local Masters participant in the 1980s and 1990s and was still playing in 2009-2010.*

Scott and Melisa Crawford – *This brother and sister duo played key roles in our boys' and girls' water polo programs of the 1970s. Scott was a member of our boys' team that won the 1973 Y Nationals. Melisa was on our girls' team that won numerous national titles. Both played in our local Masters polo program during the 1980s and assisted with our unique inner-city program of the 1990s. Unfortunately, Melisa passed away not so long ago. Scott remains a solid supporter of our Alumni Club.*

Dee Dee Dave – *A strong-armed shooter, she starred on our team that brought home the silver medal from the 1975 Junior Olympics, earning Junior All-America honors that same year. She was on our team that won the 1976 Women's Junior Nationals and participated with us at the 1977 World Women's Club Championships. As a collegian, Dee Dee played for Doc Hunkler at Slippery Rock University. In more recent years, she's played Masters water polo in Charlotte while serving as a swimming coach there.*

Tricia Derrough – *A teammate of the just-mentioned Dee Dee Dave, she was a good all-around player who shared the same accomplishments as Dee Dee, i.e., a silver medal from the 1975 Junior Olympics and gold from the 1976 Women's Junior Nationals, Junior All-America acclaim, and participation at the 1977 World Women's Club Championships. Tricia has continued to play*

3

Masters water polo in Asheville over the years and has been one of the leading advocates of our Alumni Club.

Rosalind Durfee – *A swift swimmer who switched to water polo, she was an excellent offensive player. Ros was a starter on our team that won the 1972 Women's Junior Nationals and placed second at the 1973 Junior Olympics. She is continuing her involvement as an Alumni Club member. Her mom, Polly, was on our Asheville YMCA Masters swim squad that won 1972 and 1973 Southeastern titles.*

Lisa and Cindy Graham – *These sisters were the leaders of our team that competed in the 1976 and 1977 Junior Olympics and the 1977 Women's Junior Nationals. Lisa was the high scorer for this team of younger girls and earned selection as a Junior All-American. Cindy was the team's goalie. Ten years later, in the mid 1980s, Lisa returned and participated in our local Masters program.*

The Hartman Family – *Without the Hartmans, we could have played girls' water polo at the Asheville YMCA, but we'd never have attained national prominence. The dad, Bob, was Athletic Director at UNCA, our small local university, and he made the college's six-lane, 25-yard, deep-water pool available to us twice weekly for practicing ... free of charge. He also let us use the pool twice yearly for tournaments that attracted entries not only from the surrounding Southern states but also from Florida, Pennsylvania, Ohio, Illinois, Iowa, Missouri, Texas, California, Ontario, and Quebec. The practicing we did in the larger college pool and the top teams we brought to our community enabled our girls to climb the competitive ladder quickly. But there's more. The four Hartman girls – Tina, Karen, Connie, Katherine – were all strong swimmers who developed into outstanding poloists, leading our team to numerous national victories. Tina was a defensive standout who was our left-handed shooter. Karen and Connie earned a combined 10 Junior and Senior All-America certificates. They couldn't be stopped by ANY of our opponents. Connie, who also was an All-American freestyle sprinter, received the MVP award at several national tourneys, including the 1973 Junior Olympics. She was named to the all-tourney team at the 1977 World Women's Water Polo Club Championships. Katherine, the youngest, was more of a distance swimmer, but she was good enough at water polo to attend the Junior Olympics. Unfortunately, Tina recently passed away, but Karen, Connie, and Katherine continue to connect with other members of our Alumni Club.*

Heather (Hines) Lockhart – *Daughter of the author, she was a member of the YMCA's swim squad and our fourth, or final, girls' water polo team, both of which won Southeastern junior championships in 1980. She was goalie on the polo team. Heather was also a Southeastern winner in whitewater kayak racing, as well as being a certified lifeguard and scuba diver. She helped her dad teach Y swim lessons.*

Susan Macdonald – *A key member of our earliest Asheville Y girls' team, she earned a gold medal at the 1972 Women's Junior Nationals and gold and silver medals at the 1972 and 1973 Junior Olympics. Susan was equally adept on offense and defense and has continued to promote healthy living and sports as the Fitness Director at the Asheville YWCA.*

Kathy (Oates) McLeod – *She played goalie on our team that was runner-up at the 1975 Junior Olympics, earning Junior All-America recognition, and came back a year later to compete with our team that won the 1976 Women's Junior Nationals. After attending college, she returned to Asheville and was goalie on a team that took top honors in the 1983 Bele Chere coed tournament. At the present time, Kathy is playing Masters water polo and teaching Splash Ball to younger children in northern California.*

Steve and Dan Moore – *These brothers helped our YMCA boys' water polo team move up the ladder nationally, from fourth place in 1971 to third place in 1972 to the Y championship in 1973. Steve was a capable defensive player who once scored seven goals in a national tournament match. Dan was a good goalie who anchored our boys' defense in 1974.*

Ed Mullis – *A beautiful butterflyer, he was one of our fastest youth swimmers in the 1970s. While attending college, he did his 'field work' with us in the Asheville YMCA Aquatics Dept., and after graduation, he served as the Y's Aquatics Assistant for one year. During that time, he became a water polo enthusiast and arranged for the 1984 Southeastern Olympic Development Water Polo Clinic to be conducted in our Y pool. Ed now coaches high school swimming in eastern North Carolina.*

The Peake Family – *Just as the Hartmans contributed so much to our YMCA girls' water polo program, the Peakes did more than their share for our boys' program. The dad, Burt, Sr., served as an assistant coach for three years and took our boys to play a number of collegiate men's teams. Burt, Jr., was the fastest swimmer on our boys' team and subsequently attended college on a swimming scholarship. He also played college water polo. Larry was a powerful presence as a hole set who at one time shared our one-game boys' scoring record with Phil Cocke (above), both popping in 10 goals. Then along came the youngest brother, Steve Peake, who could do it all in the pool. He scored no fewer than 18 goals in a single game against a reputable New Jersey team, a national YMCA record that still stands. All three Peake boys were Prep All-Americans, Burt, Jr., in 1971 and Larry in 1973 and Steve in 1975. Burt and Larry continued to play Masters water polo at the Asheville YMCA in the 1980s, while Steve, a graphic designer, has helped this author immensely in recent years with my writing efforts.*

Dan Pierce – *One of our several outstanding goalies, he followed in the footsteps of All-American George Russell (below) and guarded the cage for our boys' team that won the 1973 YMCA Nationals. Dan played on the champion intramural team at Western Carolina University and, after returning to Asheville, participated occasionally during the 1980s and 1990s in our Masters program.*

Laura and Page Pless – *These two talented sisters moved from competitive swimming to water polo. Laura was a member of our 1971 and 1972 Junior Olympic teams. Page played on our 1972 and 1973 JO teams. Both girls earned gold and silver medals. They were on our team that won the 1972 Women's Junior Nationals, with both receiving all-tourney honors. Both were selected as Junior All-Americans. Page kept on playing for many years thereafter and was a vital member of our team that won at the Women's Senior National level. She was a Masters participant in the 1980s. The Pless parents were solid supporters of our efforts, and they continue to contribute to the Y even today.*

George Russell – *With excellent lateral movement, he was a wonderful goalie for our boys' team in 1971 and 1972. He received all-tourney honors at the 1972 YMCA Nationals and was subsequently named to the Prep All-America lineup. George then*

6

enrolled at Duke University and played goalie for the Blue Devils' club team. He came back to play for the Y at the 1975 Southeastern AAU Championships.

Margaret (Boyd) Schutrumpf – *From the beginning of her water polo career to the end, she was one of the best women's goalies in the country, earning Junior All-America acclaim twice and Senior All-America recognition thrice. At the 1975 North American Women's Indoor Invitational, attended by teams from the East Coast, California, and Canada, she received the MVP award. In her final game, in 1977, against one of the premier teams in the U.S., she blocked 16 of the 18 shots taken at the goal she was defending. That says it all. (Yes, Asheville won, 3-to-2).*

Susan Sessler – *If there's one word to describe this young lady's career in water polo, it'd be Unsung. Though small in stature, she was a tiger on defense while participating on our Asheville teams at almost every Junior and Senior Nationals for half-a-dozen years, culminating with the 1977 World Women's Club Championships. Seldom noticed, Susan finally received Honorable Mention Senior All-America acclaim.*

Corey Sims – *He was another YMCA player who too often performed in the shadows, rarely receiving recognition. He was a swift swimmer who relied on finesse to succeed in water polo. As his coach, I'd describe Corey's playing as smooth. He was a starter on our boys' team for three years, covering on defense and advancing the ball on offense, and he contributed to the team winning the 1973 Y Nationals. He was one of several members of the team who continued to play Masters water polo at the Y in the 1980s.*

Elizabeth (Jeter) Trask – *Starting out on the Y's 'B' swim squad as an 11- and 12-year-old, Elizabeth demonstrated the highest qualities of commitment and determination when she turned to water polo. Playing the hole set spot and continually battling for position in front of the opposing goal, she established our club's one-game scoring record for women and girls by powering in nine goals in the championship game of the 1972 Junior Olympics, receiving the MVP trophy as Asheville grabbed the gold. Altogether she was a three-time Junior All-American and three-time Senior All-American, earning several other MVP awards in national and international competition before concluding her water polo career at the World Women's Club Championships in 1977.*

The Wiegman Family – *Whenever the YMCA boasts about being a family-oriented organization, the Wiegmans serve as a perfect example. The dad, Jan, an architect, helped design the Downtown YMCA facility in Asheville. The five children were all enthusiastic participants in the Y's aquatics programming. Becky and Monique were on the swimming and water polo teams. They also lifeguarded and helped teach children to swim. Monique competed in the Junior Olympics. Vincent was a swift swimmer and a left-handed shooter in water polo. He and Becky played intramural polo in college. Peter was strictly a swimmer who was best in the backstroke. George, the youngest, who suffered from a serious heart condition, found his place in the pool as a shallow-end goalie. Sadly, George died at the age of 34, but the four other Wiegmans have had highly successful professional careers.*

Beth Williams – *Influenced by her mother, who was a long-time YMCA, YWCA, and Red Cross swimming/lifesaving instructor, Beth was a reliable and all-around aquatics performer. She was on the Y swimming and water polo teams and also lifeguarded and taught youth swim lessons. On several occasions, she and her family members provided lodging in their home for poloists from visiting teams.*

Debbie (Robinson) Wilson – Looking for *a star athlete who's excelled at several sports? Here she is. Debbie played nationally and internationally on our championship girls' water polo teams during the 1970s. She continued to play Masters polo and was on the team that copped our local Bele Chere coed tournament in 1983. Over the years, she's won major U.S. titles in Masters swimming and triathlon. She's also been a biker and a whitewater kayaker. Debbie helps coach the swim squad at a nearby high school. Have I mentioned that she's been an Olympic Torchbearer? And that she's one of the primary promoters of our Asheville YMCA Water Polo Alumni Club? What a gal.*

Moving from our bona fide athletes of the past to the fictional water polo picture portrayed in this novel, I thought it would be easy to find a make-believe college in California for Sandy Scott, the book's main character, to attend. I was wrong. I'd never heard of a Golden Gate Community College, but after enrolling Sandy there, I discovered there was indeed a Golden Gate University. Much to my amazement, I learned it had evolved from a night school started by the San Francisco YMCA in 1881. After the City was destroyed by the Fire of 1906, the Y continued operating the school, using tents for awhile. In 1923, the YMCA school was incorporated somewhat separately as Golden Gate College but remained in the Y facility until 1968. It became a full-fledged university in 1972 and now occupies its own buildings, where at present it is mainly a graduate school, specializing in Law and Business. Nonetheless I decided to keep Sandy at Golden Gate *Community* College, a fictional two-year school.

A similar situation popped up when I had Sandy transferring to another pretend school, Western California University, to complete his education. I'd never heard of such an institution, but again I discovered that it existed. Sort of. There's actually a University of Western California in Los Angeles that teaches English as a Second Language, Real Estate Practices, Accounting and Bookkeeping, and Nursing. There's also a California Western School of Law in San Diego and a Western University of Health Services in Pomona. My gosh. Once again, I kept Sandy where I'd placed him, at make-believe *Western California University.*

There's nothing fictional, however, about the YMCA that exists in the mountains of Western North Carolina. It's where I worked from 1969 through 1996 and where I, at the age of 81 as I write this, still go to swim thrice weekly. Originally named the Asheville YMCA, it became the YMCA of Asheville and Buncombe County, and in recent years, the organization has expanded into three other counties and is now known as the YMCA of Western North Carolina. This Y did indeed have a championship water polo program in the past. As I stated in the opening sentence of the Introduction, this novel is about what's happening now, in the present time, as Sandy returns home from California, and it's partly factual, partly fiction. Sandy and his family members and friends and the youngsters on his team are all make-believe. But some of the Y staff members are real people. This shouldn't detract from the story, which is about a young man who tries to revive a

9

defunct water polo program by recruiting a group of eager 11- and 12-year-olds to learn the sport from the bottom up.

Sandy takes his team to a tournament in a Philadelphia suburb in chapter eight. From a factual standpoint, there's outstanding water polo being played in that area, with a so-called Main Line tourney sanctioned by American Water Polo conducted each spring for 12-and-under participants. While serving mostly local teams, it's open to entries from other cities and states. There's a Wilson High School that has a large, deep pool and one of the best swimming and water polo programs in the U.S. Ed Haas of AWP and School Superintendent Rudy Ruth and Coach Tom Tracey from Wilson gave me good guidance.

Likewise there's a Grier Laughlin tournament held each November in Colorado. Like the aforementioned Main Line event, it's mostly for local teams but attracts entries from elsewhere. I'm appreciative of the Boulder Water Polo Club's CeCe Bloomfield for taking time to check my facts when, in chapter 11, I send Sandy and his team to the Grier competition. As for Coach Dave Maynard who brings a 12-and-under team to this event, he's a real character who resides with his family in Gillette, Wyoming.

There's also a National Water Polo Training Center in Los Alamitos, California, and just this past year, our U.S. men's national and Olympic team has started practicing daily in the beautiful three-pool outdoor aquatic complex at the Santa Ana YMCA in southern California. Hard to believe, but true.

I want to recognize six long-time friends from the disciplines of swimming, water polo, and whitewater kayaking who've given me continuing support over the years and kept me on the straight and narrow. They're Andy Burke from California, Janice Krauser and John Spannuth from Florida, Paul Barren from Pennsylvania, Tom Sullivan (Sully) from Minnesota, and Peter Kennedy from Vermont.

Special appreciation goes to two friends from the YMCA who've played key roles in promoting water polo, both directly and indirectly. They're Randy Bugos, President/CEO of the 10-branch, $20-million-per-year YMCA of Coastal Georgia that's headquartered in Savannah, and Ken McGartlin, now semi-retired from the Y and serving as President of the International Aquatics and Sports Foundation that's situated in Panama City, Florida.

On the home front, I wouldn't be what I am, where I am, and who I am without the support of my immediate family. This includes my wife Lee – she's a Star performer in choral singing, and we'll be celebrating our 60th wedding anniversary in 2015 – and daughter Heather and grandchildren Crystal and Charlie. As they say, love is the bottom line.

Returning to the story at hand, let me express appreciation to Brad Tirey, the Supervisor of Publishing at AuthorHouse, for guiding me through the process, and to Don Jedlovec for providing the cover photo. Brad is a former high school and college swimmer who went out of his way to be of assistance. Don is a well-known nature photographer in northern California who in recent years has branched out to cover various sports, including water polo. Check out his web-site at www.jedlovec.com.

Finally, remember what so many other writers have said: don't let the facts stand in the way of telling a good tale that tries to impart important values and virtues. I hope this is what I've managed to do in the pages that follow.

CHAPTER ONE

CALIFORNIA CHALLENGE

Everything had changed, Sandy realized, even more than he'd expected. Coach Dan Dillon had departed, as had his replacements, Coaches Guyer and Stranahan. And then Coach Griffin had come and gone. She'd been followed by Coach Kiki. The YMCA had a good reputation for developing swimmers going back as far as the 1960s and 1970s, and despite the turnover in coaches, the Y was still producing national champions, five of them in recent years, plus several national runners-up.

Sandy wasn't one of the champions, but he'd won his share of races. Then, six years ago, he'd taken off, leaving the mountains of Western North Carolina for what he anticipated would be a more exciting life in sunny California. I don't regret going, he thought, but California had started to wear thin. It wasn't nearly as glamorous as he'd envisioned. I'm glad to be back home, he felt. Back home!

Despite the coaching changes, the old Downtown YMCA Aquatic Center remained about the same, he acknowledged as he looked around. Two side-by-side pools, one with cooler water for swimming laps and youth instruction and swim team practices, the other with warmer water for aquatic fitness and therapy classes and family swim sessions. As he sat at poolside, there were indeed a few lap swimmers in the one pool and an arthritis class in the other. Each pool was guarded by a college-age lifeguard wearing a white shirt and red shorts.

Sandy smiled. He'd done some lifeguarding here himself during his high school days. So maybe things hadn't changed that much.

But he knew that wasn't totally true. In addition to the older Downtown branch, the YMCA had expanded in recent years, adding fancy facilities in three neighboring counties plus two new branches right here in town. One was a fitness center to the North. The other was a large full-facility branch to the South, complete with a nice six-lane pool. This was now the headquarters of the Y's youth swim squad, nicknamed the Piranhas, where the newest head coach, Kirk, had his office. He was doing an excellent job, Sandy had heard, increasing the team membership to nearly 150 youngsters, ages eight to 18.

"Don't I know you?" Sandy's reverie was interrupted by one of the lifeguards who had approached him. "You look familiar."

Sandy looked at the lifeguard who was female – definitely female – and cute – very cute. "I used to live here," he replied.

"Weren't you on the swim team?"

"Yeah, I pretty much grew up on the team, from the time I was a little kid."

"What's your name?"

"Sandy. Sandy Scott. What's yours?"

"Kristina. But everyone calls me Kris."

"I think I prefer Kristina. You look like a Kristina. Regal."

The young woman laughed. "And you look like a Sandy with your blond, wavy hair. Didn't you move away from here?"

"Yeah. When I graduated from high school. Six years ago. I went out to California. To seek my fortune." He hesitated. "Well, not exactly. Actually I went there to enroll at a community college. I wanted to play water polo in college, and California has the best water polo in the country. By far. So I thought I'd give it a try."

Kristina asked, "How'd you do?" But before Sandy could answer, the other lifeguard on duty called out. She turned and said, with a smile, "I gotta go, but I hope to be seeing you again."

"You will. I'm now back here, back home, for good."

Sandy watched the young lady walk away and thought to himself, some things never change. Boy meets girl. Boy likes girl. Boy hopes girl likes him.

* * * * *

The town *had* changed, though. It was larger, busier, with the roads much more crowded than he remembered. Of course, he reminded himself, it still wasn't nearly as hectic as the San Francisco and Los Angeles areas, where he'd spent his recent years. And the surrounding mountains remained as stolid, as impervious to change as … well … as the YMCA's long-time dedication to helping members grow in spirit, mind, and body.

At dinner that night, sitting around the table with his family, Sandy said, "I'm happy to be back home, and even though there's been a continuing change in swim coaches, the YMCA seems to be the same."

"Yes," his grandfather Nelson replied, "I recall going to the Y when I was a youngster myself. At that time, the Y's motto was something like 'building boys is better than mending men.' There were a lot of programs for kids, but mainly boys. One of the best was called the Clean Life Club. It was supervised by a man named Seth Perkinson. We had about 1,200 boys participating, and there was an emphasis on Bible-reading and baseball. We did some swimming in the old Y pool, too, but it was done to clean off the sweat and grime," he laughed.

"Then the Y started serving women and girls," said Sandy's dad, Brian. "They had to change their motto. It became something about being a Judeo-Christian organization. Here in our community, this meant more service projects and reaching out to help those in need. Racial segregation was ending, and I remember the Y integrated its facilities and programs. Someone observed that we may have been the only YMCA in the country to have a Jewish man as president of the board of directors and a black woman as vice-president."

"I guess the motto nowadays is contained in four words," chimed in Sabrina, Sandy's young sister, as she dished up more mashed potatoes for herself. "Caring. Honesty. Respect. Responsibility." She gulped down a mouthful and added, "We hear those words mentioned frequently at our Piranhas practices."

"Can I have another pork chop?" Sandy asked.

His mother, Carrie, nodded and turned to Sabrina. "How was practice today?"

"It was okay," the 17-year-old girl shrugged. "We did about 3,000 meters altogether in the long-course pool."

"Do the kids play as much water polo as we did in the past?" Sandy wondered.

"I don't think so. You and Bryce Bennett and some of the other boys could play really good water polo. You took it seriously, and I remember you coming home with bumps and bruises. Nowadays we play only for a few weeks during the off-season, and it's much more relaxed. Even sloppy at times. But our concern at the moment is closing out the summer season on a strong note."

"Uh-huh," Sandy chuckled. "I remember all those swimming practices when I was on the YMCA team. We worked hard, so hard that some of us tended to get burned out. I stuck with it because the coach at that time let us play water polo amongst ourselves every Wednesday afternoon. That kept me and several others going. Of course, I enjoyed attending the YMCA Short Course Nationals at Fort Lauderdale. It was cool visiting the International Swimming Hall of Fame there."

"So what are your plans now?" his mother asked. "Have you decided?"

'I'm still not sure. I always had this dream about making the national water polo team, maybe even going to the Olympics."

"Well," said his dad, "you gave it a shot by going out to California."

"And I have no regrets," Sandy said. "I met many wonderful people and had a great time, both at school and in the various pools. The Californians treated me as one of their own, for which I'm grateful. As a result, I'm still enthused about water polo. Maybe I can teach the sport here, at the YMCA. But," he added thoughtfully, "I don't want to interfere with what the swim team is doing."

"Works for me," Sabrina said with a smile.

* * * * *

Later that night, while lying in bed with his arms folded behind his head and listening to rock music on the radio, Sandy reminisced about his days in California. After graduating from high school, he'd headed out west, to Golden Gate Community College. It was a small two-year school – they were generally called junior colleges or technical colleges in other parts of the country – with a strong water polo program. There were over 40 community colleges in California that played polo, and Golden Gate usually challenged for the state championship. Some of the school's grads had even gone on to compete for the 'big four' in water polo – Cal Berkeley, Stanford, UCLA, and USC.

That had been Sandy's dream, to become good enough at the community college level to then play for a larger university, with perhaps the national team and Olympics in his future. But he knew it would be difficult, that he had two strikes against him. First, he had no formal high school experience in water polo, having played only at the local YMCA during his swim team practices. He was good at water polo, really good compared to the other swimmers in the area. But the California kids had been participating in well-organized high school and club water polo for three, four years. Many had started even earlier, as 11- and 12-year-olds in the Junior Olympic program. They'd had great coaching and knew the fundamentals of the game. They knew each other's strengths and weaknesses.

Second, going to a community college in the San Francisco Bay area was expensive for an out-of-state student, so Sandy had to work part-time. During the school year, he'd taught swimming lessons at a YMCA two afternoons weekly while most of the other Golden Gate water poloists were practicing, and in the summertime, he'd added lifeguarding to his teaching duties.

Despite having these two strikes, Sandy was determined to succeed. He was a strong swimmer, having qualified twice for the YMCA Nationals at Fort Lauderdale, Florida, and at 6-2 and nearly 200 pounds, he wasn't easily pushed around in water polo competition. His former Y swimming coach had said, "Sandy, you're fast and tough. You handle the ball extremely well. You're smart. You just need to have more game experience."

Thus with his parents' blessing, Sandy enrolled at Golden Gate. He studied hard, and he enjoyed his work at the Y, and he learned what *real* water polo was all about. As a member of the Big Eight Conference, Golden Gate played a rugged schedule, taking on such two-year schools as American River, Cabrillo, Delta, DeAnza, Diablo Valley, Foothill, Fresno, Merced, Modesto, Ohlone, Sac City, Santa Rosa, Sierra, and West Valley. They scrimmaged against the 'B' teams at Cal Berkeley and Stanford. At the end of each season, as Sandy knew from having studied the situation in advance, they almost always placed high enough in the Northern California Community College tournament to qualify for the State Championships, where they met the top teams from Southern California.

At the start of his freshman year, Sandy sat at the end of the bench, earning a spot there only because the coach took pity on someone who'd come all the way from Western North Carolina to California to attend a community college. He watched, he listened, he learned, and eventually he was inserted into the games as a fourth-quarter substitute. With his size and speed and hustle, he was a good defensive player, and toward the end of the season he moved into the starting lineup. He needed to improve on his offensive skills, mainly his shooting, and the coach, Tyler Trent, said, "Sandy, you have plenty of potential. I suggest you stay here in California in the summertime and, in addition to your Y job, play on one of the club water polo teams. This will keep you moving in the right direction."

That was the path Sandy had pursued: collegiate water polo during the school year and club water polo every summer, while continuing to teach and lifeguard part-time at the YMCA. He returned home to the mountains of Western North Carolina only at Christmas. In his sophomore year at Golden Gate, the team had advanced to the State Community College finals, only to lose in the championship game to always-powerful Long Beach City College. But Sandy had scored twice in the disappointing loss, indicating that his offensive abilities had improved considerably.

After the title tilt, an older, curly-haired gentleman approached him and said, "Son, you've got what it takes. Keep playing!"

"Who was that?" Sandy asked Coach Trent.

"That was Monte Nitzkowski. He's now retired, but he was the Long Beach City coach many years ago. He also was an Olympic swimmer and five-time Olympic men's water polo coach. He knows what he's talking about, so if he complimented you, it's quite an honor."

Be that as it may, Sandy wasn't recruited by any of the 'big four' teams of university water polo. So he selected another school, Western California, located in the hill country that reminded him of Western North Carolina. He played water polo there his junior and senior years, graduating with a degree in Recreation Administration, as he wanted to work for an organization such as the YMCA. But before that, he wanted to try-out for the national team and maybe, hopefully, eventually, the Olympic team. He knew his chances were slim, but he was now 6-3 and a steely 220 pounds. He was fast, tough, and he'd proven himself by playing four years of collegiate ball, competing against many of the best poloists in the U.S. He told his parents, "I came to California to become the best I could be in water polo. I'm getting there, slowly. Now I need to take a shot at the next level, the top level."

He'd moved to Los Angeles, where he kept on working part-time for the YMCA and devoted most of his energy to practicing at the National Water Polo Training Center in Los Alamitos. There he met most of the sport's leaders. All were supportive of the efforts that he and a few other trainees were putting into the program at the National Center. The coaches reminded him that other non-Californians such as Brad Schumaker from the Baltimore area and the Wigo boys from south Florida had subsequently made various U.S. men's national teams. A young lady from Michigan, Betsey Armstrong, had recently been goalie on the U.S. women's Olympic team. "Yes indeed, Sandy," the coaches told him, "it can be done."

But not easily! Sandy was practicing daily with the best of The Best, yet he felt he was simply 'paddling along' in the pool as he tried to keep up with athletes who were even swifter and stronger than he was. Most had been on national and Olympic teams in the past. The U.S. men and women had both brought home silver medals from the 2008 Olympics in Beijing, China, and the ladies had earned the coveted gold medal at the 2012 Olympics in London, England. Many of these Olympians were still in training for the 2016 Games in Rio de Janeiro, Brazil. Some had even given up their participation in the European pro leagues in order to train with their American teammates at Los Alamitos.

"It's hard to see how any players could be better than our top U.S. men and women," Sandy wrote in a letter to his parents. "Our facilities are excellent. The coaching is superb. And as big as I am, many of our water polo men are even bigger, several of them going 6-5, 6-6, and 6-8. They're not skinny, either. They lift weights every other day and swim hundreds of laps. Most are fast. The U.S. Olympic men's team captain goes :22 for the 50-yard freestyle from a push-off start. Their ball-handling is almost beyond belief. I ended up being a Community College All-American while at Golden Gate and then played pretty well for two years at Western Cal, and I thought I was getting good. But frankly, I can't keep up with these guys."

That was the truth, Sandy realized once again as he lay on his bed at home, revisiting his years in California. He had no regrets about going out west. He liked California and the Californians. Mostly they were friendly and open-minded, and despite being a North Carolinian, he and his Southern accent were readily accepted without any questions being asked. For awhile, he thought he'd stay there. He liked San Francisco a lot, but it was too expensive to live there, especially on the salary of a YMCA worker. He didn't like Los Angeles as much. It was too urbanized, too overcrowded, too hectic, too smoggy. Not a place where he wanted to settle down. So at the age of 24, he'd come back home.

Yes, he'd returned home. To what? To his family, for sure, and that was a definite plus. But what else? His high school friends had scattered. His Y swim coaches had departed. It was almost like starting over again. After flicking off the radio, he tossed and turned in his sleep for several hours before awakening abruptly. It remained dark outside. What had he been thinking? Or dreaming? Ah, yes, it was about playing water polo at the YMCA when he was a teenager. That had been fun and had led to his California adventure. The Y was still there, so maybe that was the place to go, to reconnect with whoever was now on the staff. What was that cute lifeguard's name? Kris. Kristina. With a smile and with his body finally relaxing, he drifted off to sleep.

CHAPTER TWO

THERE'S NO PLACE LIKE HOME

The girls were gathered in a group at a corner of one pool, giggling and casting overt glances at the tall, powerfully-built young man who stood at the opposite end of the Downtown YMCA's two-pool complex. They were young 11- and 12-year-olds, waiting for the lap pool to clear out so their swim team practice could start. The lifeguard, Kristina, walked over to the girls. "What's so interesting, ladies?"

The giggling continued. "Who's the guy down there with Coach Kiki?"

"His name is Sandy Scott. He used to be on the Y swim team here. Then he went out to California to attend college. I understand he became a good water polo player, even an All-American. He tried out for our U.S. men's Olympic team but didn't quite make it. Now he's back home."

"Is he going to help coach us, do you think?"

Kristina shrugged. "I really don't know. You'll have to ask Coach Kiki."

"Is he married?" one of the girls inquired.

"I'm wondering that myself," Kristina admitted, "but I don't think so."

At the opposite end of the pool, Sandy was finishing his chat with Coach Kiki. She'd taken over as the Swim Team Director when Coach Griffin left for Delaware, and under her supervision, the Y team had placed as high as eighth nationally, out of more than 600 Y swim squads. Several of her star athletes had accepted college scholarships. But just recently, Coach Kiki had decided to concentrate on working with the younger swimmers, so a newcomer, Coach Kirk, had been brought in to serve as Swim Team Director and head coach.

Kirk had been a high school and college All-American swimmer, and after a few years of coaching elsewhere, he'd been recruited by the Y in this mid-sized mountain town. He'd also played water polo in his younger days.

In talking briefly with Coach Kirk over the phone and now with Coach Kiki in person, Sandy had emphasized that he didn't want to do anything that would interfere with their outstanding competitive swimming program. "Here's my plan," Sandy said. "I want to take youngsters from the Y's regular learn-to-swim classes who do *not* want to be on your swim squad, or they're simply not good enough, and introduce them to water polo."

"What ages are you talking about?" Kiki asked. "Is it the Splash Ball program I've heard about?"

"Splash Ball is for youngsters 10 and under. It's once weekly, and easy. I prefer to work with those a little older, the 11- and 12-year-olds, with two or three practices weekly. Then, if we have some success with the program and can keep it going for a few years, we'd pick up the pace for the 13-, 14-, and 15-year-olds and start competing. But that's in the future. I want to emphasize that this would be separate from the YMCA's swim team. In California nowadays, competitive swimming and water polo are generally considered to be two different sports. That's what I envision here."

"I think that would be okay," Coach Kiki consented. "But keep me and Coach Kirk informed." She turned to the young girls at the opposite end of the pool and shouted, "Time to stop talking and start swimming. Get going." The 11- and 12-year-olds plunged into the pool and began churning away.

Sandy sat on the poolside bench and watched the girls for awhile. They were very good, he realized, and had benefited from competent coaching. With them as a nucleus, he could put together a good group of beginning-level poloists. But no, he didn't want to interfere. He'd have to find his players elsewhere.

* * * *

It wasn't exactly what he'd planned to do after graduating from college with a degree in Rec Administration. Here he was, a 24-year-old living at home again. His parents didn't seem to mind … MUCH … and younger sister Sabrina was enthused about his reappearance. Because she was seven years younger than he was, she'd never figured prominently in his life when he was growing up. When he went away to college six years ago, she'd been a bratty 11-year-old, just joining the swim team at the Y, and he was a star performer. They'd been civil to each other in the past, but distant. Now it was time for them to get reacquainted.

It was Sabrina who'd told him about the job at the Downtown YMCA. "They've posted an opening for Head Lifeguard. It's an important position because they've had a constant turnover of guards. They need someone with authority, like you, Sandy, to give the lifeguarding situation the stability it deserves."

Thus Sandy ended up going through the interview process with Tina and Lydia, two members of the YMCA staff. Tina was the Director of Sports; Lydia was the Director of Aquatics. They were enthused about the possibility of having someone with his qualifications heading up the lifeguard corps and tentatively offered him the position, starting at $10.00 per hour, provided he could pass a drug test and a few other requirements. Sandy wasn't one to haggle – it wasn't his style – but he had a couple of demands of his own. "I have a college education," he said, "and I grew up in this YMCA. In addition to being on the swim squad, I lifeguarded right here in the Downtown Aquatic Center, so I know what it's all about. More recently, I taught swimming at a couple of Ys in California, and I have the latest lifeguard certifications. I promise to work for one year as the Head Lifeguard, but I won't accept less than $11.83 per hour. That's the proposed minimum wage here in town. I want 40 hours of work weekly and medical coverage. That's very important to me. I'd like to run a water polo program for Y kids, which I'll do in my spare time and free of charge. I've already cleared it with the swim team coaches. So think it over and let me know."

Initially his requests were rejected. He started looking through the newspaper for other jobs. Then the phone rang and he was told the YMCA has accepted his proposals. When could he start? "Next

Monday," he said, "and I want to schedule an afternoon meeting sometime next week with our current lifeguards."

Sandy had never been one to sit idly around. He thought the Head Lifeguard should be like a coach, spending half his time on the deck, working as a guard himself, and half his time supervising the other lifeguards. Taking up the job in the busy summertime, he spent a month getting things organized, working eight hours daily from Monday through Friday and then going to the Downtown YMCA at least once each weekend to make sure his lifeguard staff was functioning properly. He had a crew of 12 guards, all part-time employees, ranging from three high school students to five local collegians to four experienced adults. There had been some turnover in the lifeguarding group, and he wanted to avoid that in the future by ensuring the current guards were appreciated and paid a fair wage for their services. "Pool safety comes first in YMCA aquatics," he told anyone who'd listen to him. "No matter what else we're doing at the Y, in aquatics or in other activities, it'll take only one accident in the pool to sour the community on our entire operation. This is serious business."

A second month passed of concentrating on his duties as Head Lifeguard before he felt comfortable turning to his *real* love, water polo. When he'd convinced himself that the lifeguarding situation was under control, he checked with Tina and Lydia, the Y's staff members who were responsible for over-seeing the sports and aquatics programs, to see about starting youth water polo.

"Exactly what do you have in mind?" Tina asked.

Sandy spent an hour talking with them about YMCA water polo. He explained that it had been a fully-sanctioned Y sport in the past with national tournaments and All-America selections. He turned to Tina. "Did you know this YMCA had national championship water polo teams in the 1970s and 1980s?"

"I've heard about it," replied Tina, "but really don't know much about it."

"I've spoken with the coach who's now retired but still lives here," Sandy said. "He's given me all the info. Apparently there were 140 or 150 Y teens who played water polo during the decade of the '70s. They were divided into 'A' and 'B' teams for the boys and varsity, junior varsity, and beginner teams for the girls. The boys won the Y Nationals once, in 1973. They defeated all *t* teams from this area plus top teams from the East a*r* They played and occasionally defeated a number o*r* ᵥ men's teams. Many of these boys kept on playing in the Masᵥ. program at the Downtown Y in the 1980s and 1990s. They hosted an Olympic Development Clinic and helped the coach at that time conduct a special water polo program for inner-city boys."

"Wow," said Lydia. "That's impressive."

Sandy smiled. "Yes," he said, "but the Y girls did even better. There were very few high school athletic teams for girls in the 1970s, so hundreds of local girls came to the Y for sports such as gymnastics, swimming, and water polo. According to the coach, the water polo girls not only won the Y Nationals three times but also the U.S. Junior Olympics, the U.S. Junior Women's Indoor and Outdoor tournaments, the U.S. Senior Women's Indoor tourney, and the North American Women's Indoor Invitational. They competed from New York to New Mexico, from Philly to Fresno, from Miami to Montreal, and even traveled one summer to Honolulu. For a finale, they represented the East Coast at the first-ever World Women's Water Polo Club Championships at Quebec City, where they played the top European women's team from The Netherlands."

"Are you kidding us?" Tina interrupted.

"I am not," Sandy laughed. "However, sad to say, the local girls lost to the much older Dutch team."

"You know," Lydia said, "I'd like to learn more about our Y water polo program of the past, but let's turn to talking about what you want to do with teaching the sport to our kids right now."

"Okay, I'm for that," Sandy consented. "But first, the coach of those boys and girls from the past has written a book with a lot of good history material. It's called *Water Polo the Y's Way*. I'll bring you a copy. Now," he continued, "let's move on ...

"The YMCA of the USA dropped half-a-dozen minor sports in 1978, including water polo. A few Ys, such as the one here, kept on playing mostly for fun, fitness, and fellowship. There was no longer any national competition for Y teams, but in an effort to at least teach the fundamentals of the game to younger swimmers, the YMCA nationally came up with an instructional program called

Wet Ball. This is what we played here on occasion when I was a youngster on the Y swim squad, and it led us to keep on playing amongst ourselves when we grew a bit older. It was great fun.

"More recently, the governing organization for the sport, USA Water Polo, has devised something similar called Splash Ball. Other countries have their own developmental programs. The Aussies call theirs Flippa Ball. The Canadians conduct I Love Water Polo courses. In Europe, where water polo is a *really* big sport with pro leagues, they have Haba Waba tourneys with thousands of children participating. I'll probably combine the skills taught in Wet Ball and Splash Ball with my own ideas and go from there."

"What ages are we talking about?" Lydia wanted to know.

"Wet Ball and Splash Ball are for very young children, ages 6 to 10, but that's too young, in my opinion. I'm looking to teach 11- and 12-year-olds, maybe the ones who aren't interested in joining the Piranhas swim squad but still want to have fun in the water. I'd like to offer two 45-minute classes per week for these kids. As I said before, I'll do it on my own time. How does that sound?"

"You don't need to be paid?" Tina raised her eyebrows.

"No. I'm being paid for being the Head Lifeguard, working 40 hours per week. Plus I'm receiving medical coverage. That's enough. I'll do the water polo as a Y volunteer. It was the Y that introduced me to the sport. Now I'd like to give back."

Tina and Lydia looked at each other. Tina said, "Sounds good." Lydia nodded. "When do you want to start?"

* * * *

Sandy knew there was a right way to do things ... and a wrong way ... and he'd been taught by his parents and church leaders and YMCA coaches to strive for the former. So he emailed the YMCA's Swim Team Director and head coach and informed him of his plans. To his informative email, he added, "As I said before, Kirk, I don't want to interfere with your swim team activities."

Kirk, who'd played some water polo himself while growing up in another state, replied almost immediately, saying, "I like water polo. It has a lot to offer. Which is why we have our swimmers playing amongst themselves for fun during the off-season. You remember how it was when you were on the swim team here. And of course, the more kids we can keep in our Y pools, the better. So you have my blessing."

Sandy also emailed the coach of the local Masters water polo team. This group operated on it own and wasn't directly affiliated with the YMCA, but they rented out the Downtown Y's lap pool and two other pools around town for their practices. They competed in the South Atlantic League along with Masters teams from Atlanta, Baltimore, Charlotte, Greensboro, Hampton Roads, Hickory, Raleigh, Richmond, and Washington, DC. More importantly, they maintained the goals at the Downtown YMCA and had purchased the caps that hung in the Y's aquatic equipment room. Sandy wrote, "In exchange for using your caps in our youth polo program, I'll personally purchase six new balls that we can share."

The Masters coach also responded quickly. "We're for anything that will promote the sport in this area. Go for it."

Sandy already had three water polo balls in his possession, each of a different size, one for men's competition, one for women's, and one for younger children. He contacted a national company to order six more balls, two of each size. The Y had several older balls lying around, so he felt comfortable and turned his attention elsewhere. The goals that were used at the Downtown YMCA Aquatic Center were not the best, he knew. The former coach, now retired, had told him they once had very good goals that were made by the local Dave Steel Company and designed specially for the Y's lap pool. The Y poloists themselves painted the goals a bright red and adorned them with discarded soccer nets. They'd lasted for 30 years – throughout the 1970s, 1980s, 1990s – but unfortunately had been unceremoniously tossed out by the maintenance department. The newer goals weren't as good and had a tendency to break apart when hit by a hard shot, so Sandy spent a Saturday afternoon repairing them.

This also gave him an opportunity to check on a new lifeguard he'd hired to watch over the family swim taking place in the warmer of the two pools. As it happened – not by coincidence, Sandy knew – the cooler lap pool was being guarded by Kristina, the young lady he'd met previously and with whom he'd kept in contact through his duties as the Head Lifeguard.

When he was finished with his repair work on the goals, Sandy spent several minutes chatting with Chet, the new lifeguard, as together they watched two dozen adults and children cavorting in the warm pool. As usual, it was a boisterous, noisy group, splashing and laughing. Then he crossed over to the cooler pool where a dozen men and women were busily swimming their laps. Up and down they went, from one end to the other. Again. And again. Lap after lap. Not much talking here. These people were fully occupied with their training. As a former competitive swimmer, Sandy studied their strokes. He picked out two who were exceedingly smooth and swift and three whom he guessed were tri-athletes, working to improve their swimming so they wouldn't be too far behind when, in actual competition, they took to the biking and running portions of their sport. The others in the lap pool were less proficient, apparently swimming just for exercise.

"How are you, Sandy?" said a voice from behind where he was standing.

"I'm okay, Kristina. How about you?"

She smiled. "You've done a good job of supervising the lifeguarding staff. The guards like to see you taking your turn on the deck, as well as the attention you give them."

"I've always enjoyed guarding. It's an important job, one that's not fully appreciated by the general public. Nor by most YMCA execs, to be honest about it. If an exec doesn't show up one day, the Y still opens its doors and goes about its business. However, if a lifeguard doesn't show up, the pools can't open. Members notice right away and voice a complaint. Furthermore, this is the most dangerous place at any YMCA. Members can drown in pools, and they do, on occasion. I've always felt that lifeguards are the Y's first line of defense against tragedy."

Kristina readjusted the rescue tube she was carrying, a device used to pull out swimmers in distress, and said, "I hear you're planning to have us do some special training in the near future."

"Yep. We'll call it the Lifeguard Games."

"What's involved?"

It was Sandy's turn to smile. "I'm not saying, except that you and the other guards should get out the water polo balls and be prepared to take on the kids I'll be teaching."

Kristina's eyebrows arose. "Water polo? For us lifeguards?"

"Yep. Can't think of a better way to train guards to do rescues than to have them battle and grapple with others in the water. Besides," he added, "in my world, everyone becomes a water polo player."

Chapter Three

SANDY BALL

"I should have asked her for a date," Sandy stated emphatically at dinner time.

"Who?" his dad asked.

His mom and sister exchanged knowing glances. Like most ladies, they were always aware of what was happening behind the scenes. Mrs. Scott said, "I've seen Kristina lifeguarding when I've taken Sabrina to swim practices. She's very cute."

"She's smart, too," Sabrina added. "But, big brother, you know that your fraternizing too closely with your staff can present problems. There's been a lot of controversy recently about swim coaches becoming intimate with their young athletes."

"I've heard about it," Sandy acknowledged with a frown. "I think the problem has mostly involved older male coaches preying on teenaged girls. I know enough to be careful. Anyway, Kristina isn't that young. She's 20 and in college. I don't see anything wrong with my dating her … if she's willing."

"Only one way to find out, isn't there?" Sabrina said. "Ask her."

"You've never mentioned much about your dating situation when you were in California," his grandfather chimed in. "How did it go?"

"To be honest," Sandy stated, "I didn't have time. What with attending classes and studying and working part-time at various Ys and, of course, training for water polo, I felt there weren't enough hours in a day as it was."

"How about church? That's always been a vital part of our family's life."

"I must admit that I didn't attend regularly. I missed it. But I tried to emphasize Christian values in the YMCA swim classes I taught. That's been an important part of the Y for me, as it was for you in the past" – he nodded in the direction of his parents and grandparents – "and I plan to continue doing this when I get the new Sandy Ball program going at the Y here."

"Sandy Ball?" Sabrina looked at her brother. "What's that?"

"It's my combination of Wet Ball and Splash Ball, taught the Sandy Scott way," he chuckled.

"Well," said his stern-faced grandmother, who wasn't inclined to speak much, "tomorrow is church. As always, that's a great way for all of us to get ready for the week ahead. We'll plan to leave the house promptly at 10:30. Together. As a family."

* * * * *

Sandy had spent several weeks advertising and promoting his new program. He passed out flyers to about 50 youngsters in the YMCA's intermediate and advanced swim classes. They read: YMCA WATER POLO IS AN EXCITING SPORT THROUGH WHICH YOU CAN LEARN TEAMWORK, TEAM TACTICS, FAIR PLAY, AND GOOD SPORTSMANSHIP. If you are ages 11 to 14 and can swim 200 yards in the Downtown Y pool (that's eight laps) and are NOT on the Y swim squad, we invite you to join us on Tuesday and Thursday afternoons, 5:00 to 5:45, to learn this exciting Olympic sport. Starts September 2nd. The first month is Free. Contact Sandy Scott at 250-POLO for further information.

He also placed several large, colorful posters that delivered the same message in the boys' and girls' locker rooms. He made sure the YMCA lifeguards and youth swim instructors were fully informed and could give the program details to anyone who asked. Finally, he had two sign-up sheets, one at the front desk in the main lobby and one in the Aquatic Center.

"You know," he told Tina and Lydia, "there are so many Y activities taking place that something like this one tends to get lost in the mix. I have my work cut out just to get Sandy Ball started with a few kids."

When September 2nd rolled around, he knew he had 10 youngsters, half boys and half girls, registered in advance. He'd taken time to check them out with the YMCA swim instructors, so he knew how well they could swim. On that day, he arrived at the Downtown Y at 10:45 a.m. He'd scheduled himself to guard in the warmer therapy pool from 11:00 to 1:00. He liked doing this as the participants were mainly older adults, many struggling with various aches and pains, and he addressed them by name. "Hey, John, good to see you... Hello, Mary, it's nice to see you again... Yes, Joyce, I too miss George, it was sad to hear of his passing... Here's a kickboard for you, Simon... Did you have a pleasant weekend, Linda?"

At 1:00, he was replaced by another guard, so he walked to the adjacent lap pool where several of the Y's Masters swimmers were completing their noon workout and heading to the showers. He knew they had to hurry back to their jobs, so he simply waved and said, "Hey there, Dave... Bill ... John... Jim... Tim... good to see you. Have a great day."

After entering the aquatic office and double-checking to make sure the lifeguarding coverage for the rest of the day was secure, he returned to the pool area and spent 10 minutes stretching at poolside. Then he dived into the lap pool and began swimming. Ah, this was refreshing, he said to himself. I need to do this more often. Get back in shape. His strong strokes propelled him swiftly and continuously from one end of the pool to the other. Half-an-hour later, when he finally had a lane to himself, he asked the lifeguard to throw him a water polo ball, and he dribbled a dozen laps, his head held high and his arms controlling the ball on the wave in front of him. He ended his workout by doing the egg-beater kick at the deep end for 10 minutes with both hands held above his head.

Time to get back to work, he thought, although swimming vigorously two or three times weekly to stay in shape was part of every lifeguard's job. At least at this Y.

Sandy showered, dried off, and donned his coaching apparel. He unlocked the aquatic equipment room and carried the two goals – one for the deep end, one for the shallow end – onto the pool deck, where he made sure they were functional, thanks to his recent repair work. He went back and brought out the caps. Sitting on a bench, he unhooked the caps, one after another, and made sure they were all usable. He knew they'd not fit snugly on the heads of younger children, but they'd have to do. Lastly, he brought out the bag of balls. He had four of them that were junior-sized, one of his own and two of the new ones he'd ordered and an older one from the Y's past. He also had a couple more that were the slightly larger women's size but could still be passed and caught and shot by smaller hands.

Then he picked up the registration sheets from the aquatic office and the front desk in the lobby and sat down to go over the names one more time. Okay, he thought, I'm ready. It's time to start playing Sandy Ball.

* * * * *

"So," asked his dad at the dinner table, "how'd it go today?"

Sandy hesitated before answering. He wanted to be positive. "It was a beginning. There were 10 kids who showed up. They all had decent strokes, but not one could swim fast. I can see why they're not on the swim team. But we did some passing and catching, and I had them take turns shooting at the goal at the deep end. Then we did some cross-pool dribbling. And finally I showed them the egg-beater kick. I think they enjoyed it."

"Sounds like you're off to a good start," said his mom.

"Yeah, but I realized that 45 minutes isn't enough time. Before we began, it took us a few minutes to get the lane ropes out of the pool, then a few more minutes to put up the goals at both ends of the pool, and then we had to stop early so we'd have time to put the lane ropes back in for the lap swimmers who were waiting. I guess I didn't do a very good job of planning."

"Didn't you remember how it was when you were a teenager at the YMCA here and played water polo on Wednesday afternoons?" his dad reminded him.

"I must have forgotten. When we played out in California, whether it was at Golden Gate or Western Cal or with the national team at Los Alamitos, the pools were all set up for water polo whenever I arrived for practice. There were even team managers who handed out the caps. All I had to do was hop in the pool."

"The YMCA is different," Sabrina said.

"Yeah," Sandy agreed. "I had the lifeguard on duty help me with the lane ropes, and I showed the kids, as young as they are, how to remove the goals at the end of practice and haul them to the equipment room. I had the youngest ones, a couple of 11-year-olds, collect the balls. When we're ready to wear the caps, I'll show them how to bring them to me and put 'em away when we're done." Smiling, he added, "At one point, I used another name for the goals. I called them cages. The kids thought that was really funny."

"No wonder you ran out of time," his grandfather observed.

"Like Sabrina said," his grandmother spoke up, "the YMCA is different, which is why our family's been such a long-time supporter of the organization. The Y teaches sharing, and I know the participants are urged to help each other."

"You're right," Sandy nodded. "When I had the kids helping me today, I mentioned the importance of being responsible, which is one of the Y's chief values."

"Well, then," his dad declared, "it seems to me that you accomplished quite a lot."

Sandy decided it was time to turn the tables. "So what did you accomplish today, dad?"

Everyone at the table turned to face Brian Scott, who laughed at the question. "Since you asked, I'll tell you," he said, and the conversation headed in a different direction.

* * * * *

"Why did you take that shot?" Sandy pointed to the 11-year-old boy who's just tossed the ball half-heartedly at the goalie, who'd made an easy block. "Your teammate on the other side was wide open. You should have passed to him."

Two months had zipped by since he'd started the youth water polo program. Progress had been slow, but steady. The number of participants had almost doubled, to 18, and he'd convinced the YMCA's staff members, Tina and Lydia, to give him a full hour of practice time on Tuesday and Thursday afternoons. "After giving the kids the first month free," he told them, "we're now charging a monthly fee, which is additional income for the Y, so please give us an additional 15 minutes." Tina and Lydia had consented. A few of the adult lap swimmers had initially expressed their displeasure, but as the weeks passed, they seemed to enjoy waiting on the deck and watching the youngsters in the pool. One gentleman, whom Sandy knew was a strong swimmer, came to him and said, "That looks like a lot of fun. I've never played water polo, but I'd like to learn." Sandy informed him of the Masters team in town and gave him the name and phone number of the Masters coach.

After practice one day in early November, he held a meeting for the parents of the water polo kids. "I appreciate your support," he said. "It's nice to see so many of you coming to the practices and watching from the sidelines. I don't mind at all. If you have any questions or suggestions, don't hesitate to contact me. If not in person, then by phone or email."

One of the moms attending the meeting raised her hand and asked, "Is this an instructional program or a competitive program? Will our kids ever play anyone else? Is there anyone else in this area for them to play?"

One of the dads added, "We know you were quite a good player yourself, Mr. Scott, and competed at the top level nationally, so are you satisfied with simply teaching beginners?"

"Those are good questions," Sandy replied, "and that's one reason I requested this meeting, so I could explain my goals and get any input that you may have. For clarification, I want to remind you that my main duty with the YMCA is serving as the Head Lifeguard. That's what I'm paid to do. I work a 40-hour week, and I enjoy doing it. If you don't hear much about the lifeguarding crew and the safety standards we've set for the Aquatic Center, that's all for the good. It means we're doing our job and no problems are occurring.

"I'm doing the water polo program strictly as a volunteer. When I was on the swim team here in the past, we occasionally played water polo. It was mostly for fun, but I became pretty good at it, good enough to go out to California, where it's a major sport, and play there. I was fortunate to play with and against some of the best players in the country. I tried out for our national team but didn't quite make it, which was okay, as my heart remained here in the mountains of Western North Carolina. I'm happy to be back home. The YMCA has always meant a lot to me, and it was the Y that introduced me to water polo, so now I want to teach the sport to any Y youngsters who might be interested."

One of the parents raised his hand, but Sandy said, "Please let me continue, and then I'll answer any questions you throw at me."

He paused and collected his thoughts. "To be honest, I haven't decided whether this is an instructional program or a competitive program. It depends on how many children enroll, and how much talent they have, and what you as parents want me to do. Years ago, in the 1960s and 1970s, water polo was a fully sanctioned YMCA sport with national tournaments and All-America selections. Our own Y, right here, had one of the best programs in the country. I shan't elaborate except to say that even after the sport was dropped by the Y nationally, the top players in town organized a Masters program and kept on playing during the 1980s and 1990s. The coach in those days, who's now retired but still living here, told me that he and his athletes did it all. After winning national championships in the 1970s, they conducted their own local leagues and tourneys in the 1980s and 1990s. They hosted an Olympic Development Clinic for the best players in this area and, at the opposite end, operated a water polo program for inner-city children as a unique way to get them in the water and learn how to swim. All of this enabled us to keep on playing amongst ourselves for fun when I was on the YMCA swim squad not so long ago."

Sandy paused again before continuing. "I'm sure this is more than you want to know, but perhaps seeing what's been done with water polo by the YMCA in the past can help us determine where we might want to go in the future. In answer to your specific question about whether there are other teams for us to play against, the answer is yes and no. There used to be two dozen other Ys in the Carolinas, Georgia, Tennessee, and Kentucky that played youth water polo. No longer. But there are Masters – that's adult – teams in Charlotte and Greensboro and Raleigh, plus several collegiate teams – and some of them are teaching children to play, just as we are. However, their programs are not YMCA-affiliated, so who knows?" Sandy shrugged, paused again, and said, "Thanks for listening. Now let's have those questions."

The hands went up, and for the next 20 minutes, the parents asked a variety of questions, ranging from the rules of the game to the food their kids should be eating to why none of the Y's swim team members were taking part in water polo. Sandy did his best to respond and then brought the meeting to a close. "Thanks for coming. Thanks for sharing your thoughts and ideas. I believe we're all in this together. Let me remind you that we have a game planned for Thanksgiving Weekend, which coincidentally happens to be my 25th birthday. I'll be dividing our players into two teams, hopefully of equal ability, and we'll play a regulation game. Information is on our web-site. If you're not going to be in town, let me know before I choose up the sides. Again, thanks for coming, and drive carefully on the way home."

* * * * *

"You've drawn a good crowd," said Sabrina Scott to her brother.

Sandy looked up and down the lap pool at the Downtown YMCA. He'd placed three dozen folding chairs along the deck, and all of them were occupied. So was the permanent bench which ran up and down the length of the 25-yard pool, with the occupants sitting elbow to elbow. In addition, several dozen others were standing at both ends of the pool. "Not bad," he acknowledged, turning to his sister. "The YMCA is mainly in the business of serving active participants and not attracting spectators. The emphasis is on personal improvement and not on sitting and cheering for someone else. Still, it's encouraging to see so many parents and others who've come to watch."

What they were watching was the Thanksgiving Weekend water polo game involving Sandy's young but eager athletes. He'd divided his players, ages 11 and 12, into two teams of nine each. There were boys and girls on both of the teams, and his sister, after attending one of the practice sessions in October, whispered to Sandy, "The girls are better than the boys."

Being a normal male, Sandy wasn't ready to believe that was true, although he knew that girls generally matured earlier than boys and had an edge until the teen years. Then the boys forged ahead, at least physically.

Now it was halftime of the Thanksgiving Weekend encounter, and Sandy gathered the two teams together and gave them some advice. To the Cougars, he said, "You're doing a good job defensively, but your passing on offense needs to be better. On several occasions, Lexie's been open in front of the goal, but you've not gotten a pass to her. Look where you're planning to pass, and then pass accurately. Put the ball in the hand of the receiver." To the Warriors, he stated, "I'm not seeing much movement out there. You're doing too much treading in one place and not enough swimming. You need to be driving to the goal more often." Then he addressed the two goalies. "There haven't been many shots taken by either side, but you've both done a decent job of stopping the shots that've come your way. When you're goaltending at the deep end, work on your egg-beater kick even when the ball is at the shallow end. Okay, gang, let's line up and play better in the second half."

Sandy turned to his sister and his new girlfriend-of-sorts who were manning the desk on one side of the pool, one serving as timer and the other as scorer. "Ready, Sabrina? Ready, Kristina?" Both nodded. With the teams correctly lined up at opposite ends of the pool, Sandy blew his whistle and dropped the ball in the exact middle. Both teams sent their fastest swimmers out to capture the ball, and the second half was underway.

As he refereed, Sandy watched carefully to see how each player would respond to this, their initial competitive experience. He knew that Lexie was the best player in his program. She also played in the community's youth soccer league, where she was a leading scorer in her age group. She has the potential to become a star, Sandy surmised, if only I can get her to work on her swimming speed. We can build our team around her. She was just turning 12, with her birthday falling on almost the same day as his. Our fates are intertwined, he told himself.

The two goalies were of equal ability, he knew from the nearly three months of practicing. Neither Nona, the girl, nor Jose, the boy, could swim with any degree of skill, but both had learned the egg-beater kick and were unafraid of a ball thrown at them as they defended the goals.

There were two swift swimmers in the game who could've, should've, been on the YMCA swim squad. They'd passed through the Y's swim classes from beginner to advanced with ease. One, Princess, had tried out for the Piranhas but didn't like it, for whatever the reason might be. Something about girls getting along with other girls, or not, so Sandy had heard. Princess happened to be black, which set Sandy to wondering. The other swift swimmer, Ellery, said he preferred games played with balls, and Sandy had seen him shooting hoops in the Y gym on occasion.

As so often happens, the parents on the sidelines were becoming noisily involved as the game moved into the fourth quarter. It was tied at 4-to-4. "Swim, Junior, swim," one mother shouted. "Don't hesitate, Ben, take a shot," a dad called out. "Look, ref, he's holding my boy," another dad insisted. Sandy, in charge of the action, both as coach and referee, had taken steps from the very beginning to eliminate any unnecessary roughness from his water polo program. While that was part of the sport when played at a higher level, he wanted his kids to concentrate on learning the fundamentals of the game. "Hands up," he always told the youngsters in his program. "No grabbing, no holding, no swimming over another player. Keep it clean." When questioned by those who knew water polo to be a more combative sport, he replied, "Normally, that may be. But I'm teaching the kids my version. It's called Sandy Ball."

Chapter Four

GUARDING THE LIFEGUARDS

"I can't believe how much progress your water polo kids have made," said Kristina, as she and Sandy walked a path alongside the river that flowed through town. They'd now gone on three dates, and here they were, enjoying each other's company on a Sunday afternoon. It was early December, and the trees were finally releasing the last of their leaves as autumn reluctantly turned into winter.

"For better or worse," Sandy replied, "I found myself pushing them more than I'd initially planned. I intended this to be an instructional program, simply a twice-weekly course that was an addition to the Y's ongoing learn-to-swim classes, but I discovered that once the ball was thrown into the pool and we began scrimmaging, my competitive juices started flowing, even though I was coaching and refereeing, and somehow this was transferred to the kids."

"I know they like to see you in the water with them, demonstrating the skills yourself."

"When I was teaching swimming at the Ys in California, I learned it was best to be in the water with the beginners. I could demonstrate, and just as important, they felt more secure when I was there, actually giving them a helping hand. So this is what I'm doing in the water polo program."

"It looks like you have several youngsters with real talent."

"Hard to tell, as they're so young, but out of the 18, I'd say we have five or six with potential. The best of the bunch is Lexie. For a girl who's just turned 12, she's a whiz. She could develop into a star in soccer or water polo or, I daresay, any sport she tries. Her parents were both athletes during their younger days, and they seem to be supportive of what I'm doing, which is a good thing. On the other hand, a couple of parents have already become a bit too pushy, which I guess is typical for all youth sports."

"You have to take the bad with the good, right?" Kristina observed.

Sandy continued with his commentary, feeling relieved to have someone with whom he could share his thoughts. "If it's basic instruction, there's usually not much debate about what's being done, whether it's in the classroom or in the pool. There's a certain curriculum to follow, plus prescribed tests to determine success or failure. This is even true in some sports, particularly those done on an individual basis, such as competitive swimming. In practice, you do a specific number of laps, and at the meets, you do the designated strokes with little or no variation. You do your thing, to the best of your ability, without having any control over the other athletes. At the end, the stop-watch tells the tale.

"But in team sports such as water polo, there are more variables than you can count. Each player has his or her own quirks, and there's room for free-lancing on every possession. You aren't limited to one lane or one stroke. In fact, the best players are those who can improvise and throw surprises at the opposing team. Then there's the challenge of putting it all together as a team, as a unit, which isn't easy. More often than not, it's teamwork that tells the tale in team sports."

The couple continued walking in silence. Kristina was wise enough to let Sandy stay immersed in his thoughts, and eventually he said, "I suppose another important factor in water polo is adjusting to the officiating. The rules can be confusing, and the referees are all different. I can tell you..." He stopped abruptly. "Hey, I'm sorry, Kristina. I didn't mean to get so carried away. I apologize. Let's change the subject."

"Okay. You haven't mentioned anything about your *real* job, serving as Head Lifeguard for the YMCA. I know you think that's important, too."

"Yeah, it's what I'm getting paid to do by the Y, isn't it?" They kept on walking for awhile, and then Sandy said, "I think we have a good group of guards, don't you?"

Kristina nodded. "Yes, we do. It must be difficult for you to keep an eye on all of us. After all, both pools need guards from 5 a.m. to 9 p.m. on weekdays and also on weekends. That's about 100 hours every week. Lydia told me it was more than she could handle with all her other duties as the Director of Aquatics, which is why she employs a Head Lifeguard to assume responsibility for the guards. I can see it's a full-time job in itself."

The husky young man at her side guided them to a bench, where they sat down. They could hear the river rushing through the rapids behind them. "Look," Sandy said, as three kayakers came into sight, deftly maneuvering their small boats to avoid the rocks and leafless tree limbs that overhung the river bank. Returning to the subject, he said, "I try to lifeguard two or three hours daily myself, and I spend another two hours every day updating the lifeguard schedule. Some of the guards like yourself, Kristina, are in school and have classes to attend. Others have part-time jobs aside from working at the Y. A couple of the ladies are married and have family obligations. One even has children. I have to take all their various needs into consideration. On occasion, one gets sick. On another occasion, one has a car that breaks down. Frequently the schedule must be readjusted. Then, of course, there's the training we do. That has to be done at a time when everyone can attend."

Sandy paused and caught his breath. "The guards are also responsible for keeping the pool decks clean, for checking the water temperature and the chlorine content and … well, Kristina, I don't have to tell you, do I?"

The pert young lady laughed. "No, I've been lifeguarding at the Downtown YMCA for four years, since I was 16. I was on the swim team before that, but I needed to earn a little money so I could attend the community college. It doesn't cost much to go there, and my parents had set aside a few extra bucks, but I wanted to cover my own expenses. I just wish the lifeguards were paid a decent wage for what we do. Without us, the pools wouldn't be nearly as safe."

"Yeah," Sandy agreed. "Our guards prevent a whole lot of accidents before they happen. It's a form of 'preventive medicine' in the pool, which most people don't fully appreciate. Even so, we're averaging one pool rescue per month, and last month the new guard, Chet, was called into the men's locker room when one of the older Y members collapsed. He administered CPR and revived the man, luckily. Who knows what would've happened otherwise?"

"So, boss," Kristina suddenly smiled, "you've had us playing some water polo at our last two training sessions. What's with that?"

"Apparently you weren't listening," Sandy chided her. "While water polo is good for exposing the guards to body contact in the water, which is a part of many rescue efforts, you also have a game scheduled against my kids during the Christmas break. You'd better be prepared."

"So who'll be refereeing? You? If so, we don't stand a chance!"

Sandy stood and stretched. "You've got that right."

* * * * *

Once again the Downtown YMCA's lap pool was jammed. It was the Saturday after Christmas, and this was the day the lifeguards were scheduled to take on the youngsters in the Y's recently-resuscitated water polo program. It didn't appear to be fair. After all, how could a team of 11- and 12-year-olds compete against a group of older, bigger, and seemingly more athletic adults, even if the youth polo program had acquired a new player, a swift-swimming 14-year-old boy who'd decided to drop from the Piranhas and play water polo. "It looks like more fun," he'd declared. Sandy had tried to dissuade him, but the boy insisted, and his parents had approved the transfer from one program to the other.

At his family's Christmas dinner, Sandy had expressed more than a little anxiety. "You know," he said with a grimace, "I hope I won't live to regret what I'm doing. I hope that the guards won't be too rough, that they'll take it easy on the kids."

"What's the purpose of the game, anyway?" his always-cautious grandmother asked.

"I wanted to do something that'll challenge the kids. With no other youth teams in this area to play against, they need something to motivate them to keep on working hard at their practices, to keep improving."

"Didn't you listen to the sermon at last night's Christmas Eve service?" his mom said, passing another helping of green beans to Sandy. "It was about having patience. Don't rush things. Let life unfold as it's supposed to do."

"I heard it. Patience isn't one of my virtues, but I'm working on it. Somehow I saw this as a good way to work with both the lifeguards, providing them with training that's different from what they're used to, and the water polo kids, giving them … well, who knows what it'll be giving them? I know I scared their parents when I announced the game would be taking place. One dad jumped up and asked how I expected 11- and 12-year-olds to compete against a group of adults."

"What did you say, son?" his dad inquired.

"I told them I'd devised some special rules to even the odds." Sandy remembered talking with the lifeguards at the end of their third water polo practice, telling them exactly what he'd told the anxious parents. "This isn't full-fledged water polo. It's Sandy Ball, which means no overt aggressiveness. Keep your hands up. You lady lifeguards can shoot with either hand, but you guys can shoot with only your off-hand. In case you've forgotten, the kids use a smaller, junior-size ball, and we don't want your mile-a-minute shots hitting one of the young goalies in the face. We want this to be a good experience for the youngsters. Also, you've said that you don't trust my officiating, that you think I'd favor the kids. I agree. So I won't be refereeing." This brought a cheer from the dozen guards gathered around him, but it turned to a groan when Sandy added, "Instead, I'll be playing on the kids' team. However, I'll be playing defense only, in front of the kids' goal. I won't be crossing mid-pool."

So now the game was being played, and it was halftime. The parents of the youth team – they were now referring to their children's activity as being a team sport rather than participation in an instructional program – were definitely more relaxed. With light music playing in the background, thanks to the radio Sandy had placed at poolside, they chatted with each other, turning occasionally to the small makeshift scoreboard to make sure what they thought was happening was actually happening. The scoreboard read Sandy Ballers 4, YMCA Lifeguards 2.

* * * * *

During the first two quarters, the youngsters had repeatedly turned back scoring attempts by the lifeguards. Whenever the guards had approached the Sandy Ballers' goal, Sandy, with his size, speed, and strength, had interrupted their attack. "I can see why he was an All-American," one parent said. "No one can get around him." When the guards did manage to get off a shot, it wasn't a strong one, as the rules being utilized in the contest required the men to shoot with their off-hands. Of the half-dozen shots they'd taken, only two had slipped by Jose and Nona, the young goalies.

On offense, the Sandy Ballers were erratic, but with no holding or pushing or other aggressiveness permitted by the lifeguards when on defense, the young poloists were able to advance the ball down the pool. The addition of Hector, the 14-year-old who'd recently joined the team, was helpful. He was a bit bigger, and having been on the YMCA Piranhas swim squad in the past, he had some speed, and the one skill he'd mastered in just a few weeks was dribbling. Whenever Sandy made a defensive stop, he passed the ball to Hector at mid-pool, who in turn dribbled into the offensive end where he passed to Princess or Ellery. If they didn't have a shot, they tried to pass the ball to Lexie, who was positioned in front of the lifeguards' goal in what was called the hole set spot. Lexie had taken four shots, two of which had been successful. Seeing that Lexie was a scoring threat, the guards had fallen back to defend her, and Princess and Ellery both had tossed in a shot from farther out.

Gathering his youngsters around him during the halftime break, Sandy said, "I'm staying in the game, but I want Hector, Jose, Ellery, Princess, and Lexie to sit out the third quarter. It's time for Ben, Beatrice, Jill, Junior, and Ryan to have a turn. Nona, you're the goalie. Now listen, everyone. This quarter we want to play really well defensively. It's important that you guard closely when the lifeguards have the ball. Don't be slack. Keep your hands up and try to interfere with their passes. Do you hear me?" The young heads surrounding him nodded. "When we have the ball, I'm going to try and throw it directly downpool to Junior, who'll be sitting in the hole set spot. Then it's up to you, Junior. You're our offense this quarter. Try to get off at least three or four shots. Aim for the top corners. Get me?" The young lad nodded. "Okay," the coach said, looking around the circle, "let's play Sandy Ball."

As the third quarter unfolded, it was obvious the lifeguards had altered their tactics. They knew to stay away from Sandy when they were on offense, and they passed the ball back and forth, back and forth, patiently waiting for him to move to the left side of the pool or the right side, and then they'd make a quick pass and shoot from the opposite side. They let the ladies do the shooting, and Kristina pumped in two goals, tying the game at 4-to-4. With the substitutes in the pool, the youngsters weren't able to muster much offense. Sandy had hoped that Junior, the best of the subs, would be able to score at least once, but he was unable to do so. The parents, who'd been cheering from the sidelines in the first half, suddenly became quiet.

In the fourth quarter, Sandy reinserted his best players into the game. They were fresh, having rested during the third period. But so was the lifeguard team, having used its substitutes, as well. The pace picked up. The referee, Keith Cartwright, a member of the local Masters water polo club, hustled on the deck from one end of the pool to the other, trying to keep up with the action. His whistle blew once or twice every minute as he signaled the various infractions. The parents started shouting again.

Neither team seemed able to score. Sandy had pulled Hector back to the defensive end of the pool, and the two of them together thwarted every attack by the guards. But the lifeguards had tightened up their defense, too, and prevented Ellery and Princess from passing the ball to Lexie. Then, with two minutes to go, Sandy surprised everyone by tossing a long pass the length of the pool, from his defensive spot to Lexie, who was sitting in the hole set position. The guards quickly doubled back on her as she was preparing to shoot, and one grabbed her arm. The ref whistled a foul and awarded the Sandy Ballers a penalty shot. Okay, Sandy thought to himself, which of the kids should I select to take the unguarded shot? Making the decision, he swam to Princess and quietly said, "It's your shot. Remember that when the ref blows his whistle, you have to shoot immediately. Put the ball in the upper left corner. Can you do it?"

"I think so."

"I know you can, Princess."

The young lady treaded water in front of the opposing cage, using the egg-beater kick. She held the ball at shoulder level, and when the whistle sounded, she reared back and threw as hard as she could. Sandy anticipated the ball flying toward the left corner. So did the goalie, who lunged in that direction. However, Princess's shot went to the right side, and despite not having much steam on it, nestled into the net. The crowd rose as one and cheered as the small scoreboard changed to Sandy Ballers 5, YMCA Lifeguards 4.

As the teams congregated at mid-pool for the restart, Sandy smiled at Princess and said, "I thought I told you to shoot to the left side."

"Well, wasn't that the goalie's left side? Isn't that what you meant?"

Shaking his head, Sandy turned to his younger teammates and urged them on. "The game is almost over, so let's play tough defense. Swim hard. Keep your head up and your hands, too."

The lifeguards tossed the ball back and forth but were unable to advance past Sandy and Hector. With the seconds ticking down, one of the guards lofted a long shot from 10 yards out. Sandy watched as the ball arched over his head. It went up, up, and then down, down. Nona, the young goalie, stretched her arms, but to no avail. The ball banged into the cage. A few seconds later, the game ended in a tie, 5-to-5.

* * * *

"Man, I'm glad we didn't play overtime," said Thad, one of the older lifeguards. "I was tired by the time the game ended. Those kids are in pretty good shape."

It was the Saturday following the water polo clash, the start of a new year, and Sandy had organized a two-hour party in one of the rooms at the Downtown YMCA. He'd invited the guards, the youngsters in his program, and their parents. The food – barbeque, chicken, cold slaw, and more – was being catered by Little Pigs, a well-known local eatery, and several of the dads had picked up the cost. Some of the moms had provided desserts of a wide variety. The Y had chipped in with the drinks. Even the weather had cooperated, as the expected snow had failed to materialize, and though it was a cold wintry day, the sun was shining.

Turning to Thad and the other guards gathered around him, Sandy said, "You've heard me say it before, but let me say it again, gang. Y'all are the best. You've done an excellent job of guarding the two pools and making the Aquatic Center a safe place. Whenever we've had a problem, you've worked with me to solve it. I'm proud to be one of you. More than that, when I asked you to learn water polo and play the kids, you were willing to do so."

"Not without some grumbling," lifeguard Chet laughed. The others nodded in agreement, and Wilbert added, "Seeing you on the deck taking your turn as a guard, Sandy, along with watching you swim the required laps for training every week, and then knowing the time you've put in on your own getting the water polo program going, well, that's certainly motivated me."

"It's the Y's way," Sandy replied. "I know that sounds corny, but it's the truth. I've been coming here since I was eight years old. Actually, my dad brought me to the family swims when I was even younger. But I started taking swim lessons when I was eight. I liked swimming, and occasionally we played some Wet Ball, and I was also involved with YMCA youth basketball and taekwondo. It wasn't until I was 13 or 14 that I decided to concentrate on competitive swimming. We had good coaches, and we worked hard, and one of the coaches let us play water polo on Wednesday afternoons. I think it was a combination of all the activities – swimming, basketball, taekwondo, Wet Ball, and water polo – that made me appreciate all that the Y has to offer."

After pausing to collect his thoughts, Sandy continued, "Then I took the lifesaving course here when I was 16, and that enabled me to pick up a few bucks." He paused again and said, "You know, the best part of it was the leadership I received from the Y coaches and instructors. They worked long hours, and they didn't get paid much, but with just a few exceptions, they were dedicated men and women. They wanted to make the world a better place, starting in our community. I suppose that's what I mean when I talk about the Y's way."

There was silence while the lifeguarding group that was gathered around Sandy contemplated his remarks. Then Kristina spoke up. "But, boss, we still haven't done the Lifeguard Games that you said you were planning to conduct."

"Hey," the Head Lifeguard replied, "be patient. That's coming in February."

With that, Sandy headed off to chat with some of the parents of his water polo youngsters. They'd all shown great enthusiasm for his coaching efforts after watching the kids perform so well against the older lifeguards. Now they, like the guards a few minutes previously, gathered around him. After listening for several minutes to their comments, he said, "Yes, you're right. The kids have done really well so far. They've learned the basic fundamentals of water polo. But I must caution you. We've been playing Sandy Ball, which as you know is a less physical form of the game than *real* water polo, which involves a lot of grabbing and holding and even kicking underwater. It can get pretty darn rough, and some kids can't take it. We're going to start incorporating the tough stuff into our practices as early as next week. So be forewarned. Your sons and daughters may come home complaining about what's happening, and there's bound to be some bumps and bruises."

One of the parents asked, "Why can't you just keep on teaching Sandy Ball?"

"For the same reason we can't keep the kids in beginner swim classes forever. They have to move on to the intermediate and advanced classes, to accept new challenges. Sports all get tougher as you move up the ladder. That's the way life is. I don't have to tell that to you parents. You know it. I see water polo as preparation for life. The relatively minor bumps and bruises suffered now in the pool will enable the kids to face the much more serious bumps and bruises that life brings to all of us. At least that's how I see it." He paused, and then added, "But that's enough sermonizing for now. Let's join the kids and enjoy some of the delicious food."

CHAPTER FIVE

THE LOVE GAMES

"I'm being pulled in too many directions," complained Sandy.

"So what's the problem?" Kristina asked.

"Well … I want to make sure I'm doing my job as Head Lifeguard at the Downtown YMCA. That's a given. After all, it's what I'm being paid to do. The youth water polo program is also important. We've taken great strides forward over the past four months, but we have a lot of hard work yet to do. Then I've been asked by the local Masters swimming and water polo teams to join their programs. They're separate, but both are good. Finally, the minister at church would like me to teach the Sunday School class for sixth graders. I told him I didn't feel qualified to do that, but he said I was good with kids and that they'd respond to my teaching. What do you think?"

The two young adults were seated on a bench alongside the river, where they'd spent time together in recent weeks. It was a cool winter day, and they were bundled up. Kristina said, "Didn't you go to the Sunday School classes when you were growing up?"

"I did indeed, and they gave me a firm religious foundation."

"I think it's something you could do. Should do. Preparing for each week's lesson will take only an hour, and you're already attending church services on Sunday, so you'd have to go an hour earlier for the Sunday School classes. That's not asking too much. And I agree with Pastor Kent. The kids would love you."

"Yeah, I like Kent, even though he swims at the Cheshire Fitness Club rather than the YMCA. I guess I'll give it some serious thought."

"There's something else you should know," Kristina said, nudging Sandy with her shoulder.

"What's that?"

"I heard Coach Kiki of the Piranhas talking the other day about having you come to a few of her practices to demonstrate racing starts. Someone told her you were always the fastest one off the blocks when you were on the Y team."

"Oh, boy. Maybe I should've stayed in California where I didn't have so many choices to make."

"You were busy there, too, weren't you? You had classes to attend, homework to do, your part-time job at the various YMCAs, plus water polo. Sounds like you're used to carrying a full load, Sandy."

The young man shrugged his wide shoulders but didn't reply. He seemed to be deep in thought, so Kristina remained quiet herself. The wind whistled through the bare-limbed trees. The water in the river behind them bubbled and gurgled. No one else was in sight. Finally Sandy spoke. "You know, I've neglected to mention one thing I'm doing that's *really* important to me."

"What's that?"

"It's you, Kristina. You're important to me. I want to make sure I have time to be with you."

With a smile, the young woman pulled Sandy close to her, and he, in turn, wrapped his arms around her. Amidst the cold of winter, they hugged. Kristina said, "I feel the same way about you."

* * * *

It was a bit frustrating, and Sandy, standing on the pool deck, forced himself to hide his annoyance. The noise from the family swim in the warm-water therapy pool spilled over to the adjoining lap pool, where he was trying to conduct a water polo practice. In the past, when he'd been on the YMCA swim squad, practicing in the two-pool Downtown YMCA Aquatic Center hadn't been so bad. The coach posted the workout, and the swimmers raced up and down the lap pool with their heads usually buried in the water. There wasn't much conversation. When the coach needed to correct a stroke, he leaned over and spoke directly, and quietly, to the swimmer. No one was bothered by the noise coming from 'next door' in the therapy pool. But water polo was different. The players had their heads up, and there was continuing verbal interplay between each other and with the coach. When scrimmaging, there was constant whistling by the coach or referee to signal fouls. Sandy found himself raising his voice time and again to make himself heard over the splashing and shouting from the family swim.

When he'd mentioned the problem to his family members around the dinner table, his dad had said, "This isn't California, Sandy, where you have huge pools with plenty of space."

His sister added, "And where water polo had exclusive use of the pool for practicing. You're not there now, big brother. You're back at the Y here in the mountains of Western North Carolina, where we have limited facilities and *everyone* is welcome."

"That's right," his mom tossed in her two cents worth. "Besides, when the parents questioned why you put the subs into the game against the lifeguards in the third quarter, I heard you distinctly tell them that *at the YMCA, everyone plays*." She continued. "That's why there are two pools at the Downtown YMCA, so the Y can serve not only the strong competitors but also the hoi polloi."

"Hoi polloi? What's that?" Sabrina asked.

"It's what we are, darling daughter," her mom replied. "The common people. The great majority. Those who aren't rich and famous."

"You know," Sandy said, "we may not be rich when it comes to money, and we're most certainly not famous, but I wouldn't trade being a member of this family for anything. And I appreciate y'all setting me straight, reminding me of what the YMCA is all about."

Those words now came back to Sandy as he stood on the deck, trying to make himself heard. "Everyone come over here," he shouted to the youngsters in the pool, pointing to a corner at the shallow end. He jumped into the water himself, and as his players gathered around him, standing on the bottom, he said, "I know it's noisy in here, so let's do it this way. At the end of each 20-minute practice segment, whether it's passing or shooting or whatever we're doing, and at the end of each quarter if we're scrimmaging, we'll take a brief break and gather here as a group, as a TEAM, in this corner. I'll be able to talk with you in a normal voice. Okay?"

Seeing the young heads nodding in agreement, he continued. "You know that we're picking up the pace. In addition to the Tuesday and Thursday afternoon polo practices from 5:00 to 6:00, we've been given lane four at the same time on Friday afternoons. We can't squeeze all of you into just one lane, so we'll have you coming on alternate Fridays. We'll be doing mostly sprints. That's short races, 25 yards, maybe 50 yards at most. With your heads up. Swimming and dribbling. You hear what I'm saying? Any questions?"

"Coach," spoke up Beatrice, "the scrimmage on Tuesday was too rough. It wasn't fun."

Sandy was prepared for this complaint. He knew that several other team members were unhappy with moving from Sandy Ball, with its rules that restricted unnecessary body contact, to *real* water polo, which was a combination of swimming, basketball, and rugby. It was indeed a rough sport, increasingly so as players moved up the ladder from age group competition to high school to college and then, for some, international action. There was no hiding from the facts, so Sandy decided to tell it like it was. He said, "It's your choice, Beatrice. For all of you," he went on, looking at the young faces staring at him, "it's a choice. We can keep on playing Sandy Ball amongst ourselves, which IS fun, or we can play water polo, which is a game that'll test your mettle. If you don't know, mettle is a word that's spelled m-e-t-t-l-e. According to the dictionary, it means courage, spirit, fortitude. Personally, I like to think of it as meaning character. So water polo is a test of your character. Yes, it's a tough game. Whether or not you want to play it is up to you. To each one of you. If you decide you don't want to play, that's okay. There are other good classes for you to take here at the Y. This spring I'll be teaching a junior lifesaving course, and I'd be delighted to have some of you enrolled. Becoming a certified lifeguard is also tough, and I'm proud to be one myself, and when you're guarding, you're responsible for the safety of dozens, sometimes even hundreds, of swimmers. So it's not easy. But it's important, and certainly worthwhile. I guess what I'm saying is that if want simply to have FUN, and that's all, you'll probably have to go somewhere else. It's your choice."

With that, Sandy tossed the ball he'd been holding high into the air with his right hand and smiled. As he caught the ball with his left hand, he said, "I've talked long enough. Let's line up at the ends of the pool and play … water polo."

* * * * *

"I understand you had a tough talk with your water polo kids the other day," said Tina, one of the YMCA's key staff members.

"Did I come across as being too demanding?" Sandy asked.

"I can only say that I've received phone calls from several parents wondering what kind of program you have in mind now that you've replaced Sandy Ball with water polo."

"Well," Sandy replied, "I've realized it was water polo that I wanted to teach all along. Apparently I've not done a good job of teaching if you're receiving complaints."

"I wouldn't say that," admitted Tina, who'd been a star soccer player herself and then a coach before assuming YMCA administrative duties. "I think you've done a remarkable job of teaching the kids. But as young 11- and 12-year-olds, maybe they've just found it difficult to make the switch from Sandy Ball to honest-to-goodness water polo with its rough play."

"What do you suggest?"

"It would be good to have the parents on your side. Why don't you hold another meeting with the parents and bring them up to date on what you're trying to do? Clarify everything, and then answer their questions. Unlike football and basketball and baseball and soccer, water polo is a remote sport that none of the parents has ever played. Very few, anyway. They don't understand what happens in a game, especially what's taking place underwater and unseen, and why it has to be so rough."

Having received such good guidance from Tina, Sandy decided also to telephone the former coach, asking him how he'd sold the sport to the Y parents in the 1970s and 1980s. "Here's what I think you should do," the 81-year-old gentleman replied. "Get in touch with several of my former players who still live around here. They're now men and women in their 50s. I'll give you their names and addresses. Ask them how they feel about having played water polo at the Y when they were youngsters. If they feel it was a positive experience, ask them to attend your meeting and speak up. Hearing something good from those who played the game here in the past will do more to convince your parents than anything you could say."

More good advice, Sandy decided, so here he was, in the meeting room at the Downtown YMCA, with quite a crowd seated in front of him. He started by saying, "I'd like to apologize to you parents for coming on so strong with your children. I suppose it's due to the fact that I was in the high-powered water polo program in California for so many years. Out there, with hundreds of teams, thousands of players, and coaches climbing over each other as they struggle up the ladder of success, it's go-go-go all the time. I realize this isn't the Y's way.

"We've had a lot of FUN in our Sandy Ball program, while also making progress. I think we can agree that it's been a success. Now the question is this: do we want to move on to *real* water polo? I thought we did. But it's not my decision alone. It's up to you, as parents, and your youngsters. Although I've discussed the situation with some of you, I need to be more open with ALL of you. So here's the story."

Sandy motioned to Keith Cartwright, one of the local Masters water polo players, who passed out forms to the parents. "You don't have to look at the forms right now. It's information you can take home with you. One thing that's shown on the forms is the ranking of sports in difficulty, done in 2011 by a national organization that measured endurance, speed, strength, agility, skill, and physicality in three dozen activities. When all was said and done, water polo was ranked first, followed by Aussie rules football, boxing, rugby, ice hockey, American football, basketball, gymnastics, soccer, triathlon, and tennis."

There was a shuffling of the forms as the parents glanced at what they'd been given. Sandy continued, "Of course, the organization doing this study was measuring the sports as they were being contested at the highest levels, not in age group competition or the Sandy Ball version of water polo that we've been playing here. But if we decide to move on to *real* water polo and continue playing for three, four, five years, it's going to become rougher and tougher. No way around it."

One of the parents stood abruptly and said, "We know you'd like to have the kids learn to play water polo the right way, Coach, but if we decide to stick with Sandy Ball, will you stick with the kids?"

Sandy closed his eyes and swept his hand across his face. Taking a deep breath, he replied, "I can't tell you how much I've fallen in love with these kids, with your youngsters. They've done everything I've asked them to do. But since one of the YMCA's values is honesty, I want to level with you, to inform you of exactly how I feel. If the decision is made to continue with Sandy Ball, I'll stick with them through the spring months. Then I'll turn the program over to Keith" – he pointed to the young man who was assisting him at the meeting – "and let him conduct the program. Keith is a member of our local Masters water polo team, and he has a good knowledge of the sport. As you may recall, he refereed the recent game between the Sandy Ballers and the lifeguards."

"What will you do, Sandy?"

"I'll concentrate on my duties as the YMCA's Head Lifeguard and will probably join the local Masters team."

Keith Cartwright intervened. "Let me tell you, we could use Sandy. With him in our lineup, we'd move up quickly in the South Atlantic Masters League. And I'm willing to work with your kids twice weekly."

"Before you reach a decision," Sandy said, "let me introduce you to some of the players from the YMCA's water polo program of the past. These men and women played on the Y's championship teams in the 1970s and 1980s. Some still live here in town, while others live in nearby communities. Some have continued playing Masters water polo here and elsewhere. Others haven't. I've asked them to come this evening and share with you their opinions of water polo, based on their own personal experiences. They started out playing for fun, just as we've done in Sandy Ball, and when they attended their first national water polo tournament, the Junior Olympics at St. Louis, they didn't win a single game. They finished dead last. But they kept on practicing hard and took on the top teams in the country from Florida to California to Hawaii, and they ended up being the best."

The parents all turned in their seats and took a closer look at the dozen 50ish adults sitting in the back row. "Let me introduce them to you," Sandy continued. Turning to the former players, he added, "Please stand up and be recognized when I call your name. Then when your turn comes to speak, keep it brief. If you can." Everyone laughed.

One after another, the former YMCA poloists stood and related their experiences of the past. All were positive, and when one woman said, "Those were the best years of my life," the others nodded in agreement. One man, looking out at the parents, said, "While water polo can be a tough game, don't let Sandy scare you away. There's definitely some wrestling that takes place in the water, both above and below the surface, but from every study I've seen, there are many sports that're more injury-prone than water polo."

Another gentleman stood and joined the reporters from the past. "Of all the games we played over a period of four or five years, I can remember just one injury, when one of our Y boys suffered a cut over his eye that required a few stitches. It was an accident that could've occurred in any team sport."

"We did have one somewhat serious injury on our girls' team," recalled one woman. "It happened when we were playing in a national championship game against a bigger, older collegiate team. One of our Y players took an errant elbow that readjusted her nose a bit. Actually, it was broken. She had to leave the game. But her injury healed quickly, and she came back to play internationally a couple of months later. I can't imagine that the competition for 11- and 12-year-olds would be nearly as rough."

The last lady in the line at the back of the room arose and, with tears in her eyes, stated, "I'll only add that being part of the YMCA family through the sport of water polo was a highlight of my life. And I happen to be the player who suffered the broken nose! It was at the women's senior nationals, in the championship game, which is a far cry from the age group competition we're talking about now. If you think Sandy can lead this program in the right direction, I recommend that you give him a chance."

There were several moments of bustling as the parents turned from watching the former players who spoke from the rear of the room to looking at Sandy, up front. Then one of the dads said, "Assuming water polo isn't any rougher than other team sports, and I suspect that's the truth, who would our kids play against, Coach? While there used to be a bunch of Ys playing in this area, you've told us there aren't many, or any, at present."

Sandy shook his head. "If you vote to play water polo, we'll face some challenges, no doubt about it. One will be finding time to practice in another pool in our community, one that's larger and deeper than the small lap pool here at the Downtown YMCA. A second challenge will be finding opponents. I can tell you there's a YMCA about an hour away that has a strong swim squad, like our Y, and a Masters water polo program, and they're willing to start a youth polo program if they know they'll have our team to play against. That's a start. I daresay we can find one or two other youth teams within a short drive if we look around."

"Then what?" the inquiring dad pursued his question.

"Can I dream?" Sandy said with a smile. "American Water Polo, which is headquartered near Philadelphia, has a 12-and-under tournament each spring. Most of the teams are from Pennsylvania, but I know they've had entries from Connecticut and New York. I'm sure they'd be delighted to have a group of kids coming from Western North Carolina. If you as parents are willing to pay for it, we can go there. It'd be a great educational trip for our kids, and they'd play against other teams of the same age."

One of the former Y players chipped in from the rear of the room. "Wherever we went to play in the 1970s and 1980s, we did some sight-seeing. When we traveled to Miami, we drove over to the International Swimming Hall of Fame and also went skin-diving in the Florida Keys. When we flew out to California, we toured San Francisco and went hiking and climbing at Yosemite National Park. When we went to Pennsylvania, which we did on several occasions, we visited Gettysburg National Park and once stopped off in Washington, DC, for two days before returning home. I remember those experiences as much as the games we played."

"That's one nice thing about doing things the Y's way," Sandy said. "While we want to practice hard, play hard, our emphasis isn't only on winning. We know that educational experiences when visiting other parts of the country are important. Even more so are the values we try to teach. My sister Sabrina tells me the swim team coaches are constantly talking about the concepts of caring, honesty, respect, and responsibility. These can be taught in the pool and also out of the pool. In fact, I've found that when the game is on, we often get so wrapped up in the scoring, the results, the winning and losing, that we forget about the values. Which is why it's sometimes better to do the thinking, the caring and sharing, the value education, away from the competition."

"Like we're doing now," one of the moms observed.

"Yes," Sandy nodded, "I'd like to think so."

"So where does that leave us?" another mom asked.

"I don't want to prolong the meeting," Sandy replied. "You've heard from some of the Y players of the past, telling you about their experiences. I've probably overstated the roughness of the sport, now that I think about it. For young children like yours, it's really not that bad. American Water Polo and USA Water Polo both conduct major tournaments for kids as young as 10, 11, and 12, just like those currently enrolled in our Y program. In Europe, there's the annual Haba Waba tourney which is for children under the age of 10. Teams from several dozen countries participate each year. These events for younger children wouldn't be happening if there was any danger of serious injuries.

"One thing that I've not mentioned tonight but which is spelled out in the forms given to you is the increased cost if you decide to go the water polo route. Playing Sandy Ball twice weekly, as we've done previously, is relatively inexpensive. Playing *real* water polo, which'll require additional equipment, more pool time for practicing, plus the cost of any trips we might take, whether near or far, can add up. There's no hiding from it. Like everything else, you have to pay the price. When I was a youngster on the Y swim team, my parents paid. When I turned 16, I had to give up some of my practice time with the team to lifeguard, so I could earn a few bucks myself. The whole time I was in California, six years altogether, I worked part-time at various Ys in order to pay my bills. That's simply the way it is."

Seeing the anxious faces on the parents in front of him, Sandy tilted his head to one side, shrugged, and said, "Let's call it a night. Take home the forms, look over the information they contain, and think about what you want to do. Discuss it with your children. When you reach a decision, contact me. You can do so by phone, or email, or by returning the detachable section at the bottom of your form, indicating whether you prefer Sandy Ball, or water polo, or something else entirely. The choice is yours."

With a scraping of chairs and a small amount of chattering amongst themselves, the parents arose as the meeting came to a conclusion. Sandy waited, in case anyone approached him. No one did. A couple of parents waved goodbye to him. Most merely turned and left the room. Wow, Sandy thought to himself, I may have turned off this entire group to Sandy Ball, or water polo, or even to the YMCA as an organization. Did I take a wrong turn somewhere?

The following morning, when Sandy returned to the Downtown YMCA for his Head Lifeguard job, he was approached by staff member Lydia, who asked, "How did it go at last night's meeting with the parents?"

"I think I blew it," Sandy said, shaking his head. Then, elaborating, he added, "I probably scared them away."

"With the warning that water polo is so rough?"

"No. I believe I overstated that situation and have now convinced them it's no rougher, tougher, than any other team sport. There are bumps and bruises, but that's life, whether in the pool or elsewhere."

"So what's scaring them?"

"The costs that I outlined in the forms they received," Sandy said. "What we've been doing, the twice-weekly practices, is affordable, just like other Y instructional classes. But when you get into competition, with more practices becoming necessary, more pool usage with probable rental costs, additional equipment, plus the expenses involved in taking trips to various tourneys, it's more than many families can afford."

"Isn't that the way it is with most youth sports?"

"I suppose. I know my folks are paying about $900 per year for my sister Sabrina to be on the Y swim squad. This doesn't include the trips. Our next-door neighbor told me he's spending $3,000 yearly for his two youngsters to take taekwondo. I know that in California, the costs for being on the various swimming and water polo clubs are even higher than they are here. But most of the families out there are wealthy."

"What do you mean by wealthy?"

"According to USA Water Polo, the national organization headquartered in California, 48 per cent of their member families have an income of more than $150,000, with another 28 per cent earning over $100,000. Compare that to the median family income here in the mountains of Western North Carolina, which is approximately $45,000. I suspect a number of our YMCA families don't make even that much."

"I'm sure you're correct," Lydia said. "That's why we have a major fund-raising campaign each year and subsidize over two million dollars in Y membership fees and programming costs for those families and individuals who otherwise couldn't afford it. This is an amazing amount."

"Yeah, I know, I know. It's the Y's way," Sandy assented, "and I believe it's the right way. But will it enable us to conduct a water polo program the way I've proposed to the participating families?"

* * * * *

The vote was conflicting. Sandy knew it would be after several of the families called or emailed him with questions. He answered them as best he could and crossed his fingers, hoping he was presenting an honest but positive outlook on what playing water polo would involve. Sitting around the dinner table at the end of the week with his family members and girlfriend Kristina, whom he'd invited to join them, he said, "Here's where we stand. We have 18 participants in the program right now. Lexie, our best player, definitely wants to play *real* water polo, and her parents are supportive. Same with Princess and Nona. So that's the really good news. It gives us a solid foundation for a girls' team, should we move in that direction."

"So, Sandy, you like the girls?" Sabrina chided him.

"Hey, I'm a normal guy. But I like the boys in this program, too. Ellery and Ben are ready to take a step up to play polo. Clayton, who's one of our poorest players, also wants to play polo, which comes as a surprise to me. The twins, Warner and Wanda, are on board, as well. Their mom is very enthused about it. Matter of fact, she tends to be too vocal and aggressive on the sidelines. Savannah is Wanda's best friend, and she says that she'll do whatever Wanda decides to do. So that gives us nine."

"What about the others?" Kristina asked.

"We're losing Hector. His parents say they can see the writing on the wall, that I'm planning to focus on the 11- and 12-year-olds which leaves Hector, who's 14, out of the picture. I'm encouraging them to put Hector back on the Piranhas swim team."

"We can definitely use him," Sabrina interjected. "He has a good attitude, and ..."

"Don't get too excited," Sandy interrupted her, "because the parents of one of the Piranhas' fastest young swimmers have contacted me and indicated they want their daughter to try water polo. I don't want to cause a conflict with Coaches Kirk and Kiki and Chris. I told them at the beginning that I envisioned the polo program as being separate from the swim squad. I still feel that way. But if a youngster wants to try another sport, whether it's basketball or soccer or taekwondo or, yes, water polo, who am I to say no?"

"Who's the swimmer?" Sandy's mom asked.

"I'm not saying, at least until she actually comes to our practices and decides it's something she wants to do. But if she jumps on board, that gives us 10."

"What about the others?"

"We're losing four for sure. Nick and Jose are bowing out, and so are Leslie and Beatrice. I'm still waiting to hear from the parents of Ryan, Janis, Junior, and Jill. Their lack of communication with me can't be good. Of these eight, I dislike losing Jose most of all. He has the makings of a good goalie, and I think he's just afraid he can't keep up with the swimming we'll be doing. I plan to talk with him and his parents and assure them that goalies are given a different workout, one that doesn't require as much lap swimming. I'll also be encouraging Nick, Leslie, Janis, Ryan, Beatrice, Junior, and Jill to take the junior lifesaving class this spring. I don't want to give up on them entirely. Who knows? They may decide to return to water polo eventually."

"So you have 10," Mr. Scott observed. "Is that enough?"

"I think we'll end up with 12. Yes, that's enough. If we can pick up two more, that'd be perfect. Besides, I have a secret plan to find a few more."

"What is it?" Kristina wondered.

"You'll find out soon enough. In the meantime, I also have to finalize plans for our Lifeguard Games, so you and the other guards better be in shape."

"You're a busy man," his sister stated.

"And you know what?" Sandy said. "I just remembered that I have a Sunday School lesson to prepare. Would y'all excuse me from the table, please?"

* * * * *

It was Saturday, February 14th, and Sandy had scheduled the Love Games for the lap pool at the Downtown YMCA. "The adult lap swimmers will complain that you've taken time away from them," cautioned Lydia, the staff member in charge of pool scheduling.

"They have 80 hours of time in the warm and cool pools every week," Sandy replied. "They can give up a couple of hours once every other month. Besides, I'm a lap swimmer myself nowadays, and I recognize there are Y programs that are just as important, if not more so, than my personal needs, especially when it comes to training lifeguards and serving kids. The other adult swimmers should be willing to sacrifice a couple of hours occasionally for the good of the organization. Isn't that the Y's way?"

Thus it was that Sandy was conducting the Love Games. It had started out being the Lifeguard Games, a test for the guards, but he'd decided to include a scrimmage for his water polo youngsters, and because it was taking place on Valentine's Day, he'd renamed it the Love Games. He'd even bought several trophies to be awarded.

The lifeguard crew of 12 had been divided into two groups of, he hoped, equal ability, and Sandy had prepared a test of 10 items. First was a 25-question written quiz which they'd taken the week before. The quiz was mainly about preventive guarding ... what needed to be done to prevent accidents and injuries from occurring. Then he had eight in-the-pool tests that the guards were taking on this Saturday afternoon. These included using a rescue tube to carry a victim, treading water, an underwater swim, a surface dive and brick retrieval, administering CPR, a rope throw, an active victim rescue from mid-pool to deck and, just when the guards were feeling exhausted, a lengthy fitness swim.

To the written exam and pool tests he added a concluding just-for-fun event, an inner-tube relay pitting the guards against the young water poloists.

At the end of the two-hour Games, he gathered the guards around him. "Everyone did well. You can stop worrying about whether or not you passed. You all did. If you weren't proficient enough to pass the written exam and the pool tests, you wouldn't be working here. I did grade everyone, however, just so you'd know if you have a weak spot or two which you can work on improving. Whoever we are and whatever we're doing, there's always room for improvement. This applies to me as well as to you. I'm always asking Tina and Lydia of the Y staff to let me know how I can improve my work as Head Lifeguard. If you have any suggestions, toss 'em at me. I won't be offended, and your job won't be jeopardized. As far as I'm concerned, and I've said this before, we're all in this together ... lifeguarding and life. Do you have any questions?"

"Will you be conducting any more Lifeguard Games?"

"Yes indeed. We'll be hiring some additional guards this summer when the two pools become even more crowded. The day camp kids will be coming every day, dozens of them if not hundreds, and we'll be offering a scuba course and perhaps other activities. At the end of the summer, in August, we'll do the Lifeguard Games again."

"But they won't be the Love Games, will they?" Thad predicted.

"No, I'll have to come up with some other fancy name. You know, now that I think about it, we may want to challenge the lifeguards at the Y's three other branches to a competition. Whatd'ya think?"

Before he received any comments, Sandy spent another 20 minutes informing the guards of the scores he'd given them for the Love Games, and at the very end, he said, "Here are the trophies for the top three. In third place, Thad. Second, Heather. First, Melvin. Congratulations. What we did today was pretty much an individual competition. If I decide we should take on the lifeguards at the other Ys in August, it'll be more of a team event. So stay in shape physically, stay sharp mentally, and let's keep the Downtown YMCA's Aquatic Center safe for all the swimmers."

With that, Sandy dismissed the guards and turned his attention to the young water poloists who'd been warming-up under the direction of Keith Cartwright, the Masters player whom he'd recruited as his assistant. Once again the pool was filled with parents who'd come to see their children in action, plus a bevy of other adults. Sandy took time to walk from one end of the pool to the other, greeting all of the parents and expressing a brief word of appreciation for their encouragement. "We couldn't have made the move from Sandy Ball to water polo without your support," he told each one. "You made it possible. What you'll be seeing today is a slightly different type of game than we played last year. There's more pushing and shoving and grabbing, and the referee will be whistling more often to signify fouls. It'll be confusing. That's why I've ordered copies of a new book, *A Parent's Guide to Water Polo*, for each family. Hopefully you'll become more educated about watching water polo while your kids are becoming more adept at playing."

As Sandy had anticipated a few weeks previously when he waited to hear from the parents of the 18 youngsters in the Sandy Ball program, he'd ended up with 12 in the switch to bona fide water polo. This included six boys – Ben, Clayton, Ellery, Junior, Warner, and Jose, who'd decided to remain on board as a goalie – and six girls – Lexie, who was the best of the bunch, plus Princess, Savannah, Wanda, Janis, and goalie Nona.

Hector, the 14-year-old, had returned to the Piranhas swim squad but told Sandy, "I won't be coming to water polo practices any more, but if you need me for a scrimmage sometime, let me know."

The roster was completed when one of the Piranhas' 12-year-olds, Delia, a swift swimmer, showed up for the polo practices. "Are you sure?" Sandy asked her and her parents. "I don't want to do anything that will disturb the swim team coaches. They have a great program that's been producing national champions, while we're just beginning." The parents had said that Delia wanted to give water polo a try, and Delia nodded.

Having concluded the Love Games with the lifeguards, Sandy now gathered his young water poloists in a group at the shallow corner of the lap pool, which had become the only way to make himself heard over the noise in the adjoining warm-water polo which, on this day, was full of family swimmers. "It's time," he told them. "Because it's important that we learn to play with each other, I'm going to change the lineups each quarter. To start, we'll have Nona, Ellery, Lexie, Clayton, Savannah, and Junior wearing the white caps and defending the deep end. We'll have Jose, Princess, Ben, Wanda, Warner, and Janis wearing the dark caps and defending the shallow end. Delia, I want you to watch with me from the sidelines. I'll put you in the game in the second quarter."

He turned to Keith, who was again serving as the referee. "Call 'em close," Sandy instructed. "They have to learn what's permissible and what's not in water polo, and they have to react to your whistle."

As the game commenced, it took only a few minutes for Sandy to see that the playing was sloppy. The passes were off-target, and the teamwork on offense was … well, the word he whispered to himself was gruesome. One reason, he realized, was that while he'd prepared a starting lineup of his best players for the game against the lifeguards, the players on the mixed teams for today's intra-squad game weren't used to performing together. That, combined with the official water polo rules that were being followed, had resulted in chaos. He let the debacle continue for the rest of the quarter although he knew the parents on the sidelines must have been viewing the action with a definite sense of dismay. This was *real* water polo? This is what we voted to do?

At the end of the first quarter, he gathered the group together again. It was obvious they were as displeased with their performance as he was. "Okay, gang, the first quarter is history, and it wasn't good. But the score is still zero-to-zero, so let's start over in the second quarter and do better. You were all right defensively, and I think you're getting the idea of how your hands and feet can be used legally in water polo. There are times when the player you're guarding has possession of the ball and you can grab and push and shove without a foul being called. Even if a foul is called, it slows down the other team. There's also more kicking allowed underwater.

"The aggressive guarding has practically eliminated our offensive efforts, though. You're not used to passing and shooting when being guarded so closely. You need to be quicker on offense. This means moving with your bodies and releasing the ball faster when passing and shooting. The defense isn't going to sit there with their hands up and let you pass or shoot, as in Sandy Ball. They've going to come after you, as you've discovered. So as I've said, move your bodies, don't just sit there in one spot, and be fast in your passing and shooting. Now that you've played one quarter of *real* water polo, you understand what the game is all about. So let's go, go, go!"

The second quarter saw some definite improvement. It continued to be a learning experience, but the youngsters did better offensively. Lexie scored on a turnaround shot from in front of the opposing goal. Warner made a shot from the left side. Ellery made one from the right side. Then, just as the quarter was coming to an end, Clayton, possibly the poorest player in the water, was left unguarded, and when the ball magically came his way, he picked it up and popped it into a corner of the cage. He raised both hands and shouted with glee. The spectators also applauded, and Sandy turned to Clayton's parents, seated not too far away, and pumped his fist.

At halftime, Sandy approached his assistant, Keith, and said, "In the third quarter, it's going to be the boys against the girls. I hope it'll turn out okay. The boys will start at the deep end, so you go down there, Keith, and spend a few minutes getting them organized. They'll be wearing the white caps. The girls will start at the shallow end, and I'll go down there and get them organized. They'll be wearing the blue caps. Let's not rush things."

Keith nodded and started walking to the deep end, signaling all the boys to join him there. Sandy went to his sister, Sabrina, who'd been watching from the sidelines, and said, "Please come with me. I need your help." Then he motioned the girls to join them at the shallow end, where he looked at the seven 11- and 12-year-olds standing in front of him. "Here's your chance, ladies. Let's play hard. My sister, Sabrina, will be coaching you in the third quarter. If you hear her shouting at you, follow her instructions. Janis, you'll be the substitute. The starters will be Nona as goalie with Lexie playing the hole set position. Princess and Savannah and Wanda, you'll be in mid-pool. When the girls have the ball, move it downpool and get it to Lexie. If she's guarded, take a shot yourselves. Delia, I want you to stay back on defense. You're fast and should be able to cover the boys when they swim toward you. Let me remind all of you that we're no longer playing Sandy Ball. This is water polo, the tough stuff. It's also the Saturday of the Love Games, so show a little love for each other and play together as a team. You can do it!"

Fearing the parents would disapprove of his showing favoritism toward the girls, Sandy had arranged for his sister to coach the girls in the third quarter while he coached the boys. His assistant, Keith, would be refereeing. The boys began the quarter with a bang. Warner and Ellery advanced the ball downpool, swimming past the girls who seemed to be shy defensively, and passed to Junior, who powered a quick shot into the girls' goal. Two minutes later, it happened again. This time it was Ben who scored. Since he was coaching the boys, Sandy shouted approval while inwardly feeling annoyance that the girls weren't doing better. He was relieved when his sister, Sabrina, called a timeout. He could hear her chastising the girls for their lack of aggressiveness. She didn't know much about water polo, but as a fierce competitive swimmer, she knew what it took to be a winner in any and every sport.

The girls responded by doing as they were told. They demonstrated good teamwork with Wanda passing to Savannah who passed to Lexie who, in turn, displayed the aggressive behavior needed by every hole set. She elbowed the defender aside, did a hard egg-beater kick that lifted her high out of the water at the deep end, and propelled a strong shot past Jose, the boys' goalie, into the cage. "Yea!" a shout arose from all the girls. "You can do it!" Sabrina yelled from her coaching position at the opposite end.

"Let's get it back!" Sandy told the boys, and they did. With good passing, they moved the ball into the shallow end, and Junior tossed up a slow but high shot that grazed off Nona's fingertips into the cage.

Once again the girls responded. When the ball was passed into Lexie, she was hammered, and Keith, the ref, ejected one of the boys for committing a major foul. This gave the girls an extra player for 30 seconds. It was a situation that Sandy had taught only sparingly during the practices, and he wondered if the girls, on offense, and the boys, on defense, would know that to do. They didn't exactly, and Princess found herself unguarded. She hesitated momentarily and then hit on a shot from five yards out. Man, she's got a good arm, Sandy realized once again.

The quarter ended soon thereafter. The boys had scored three goals, the girls two. More important than the score was the fact that the playing by both sides had been fairly decent. Not so in the fourth period, however. He reassembled the teams into a coed mixture, and as the players were becoming weary, it was again chaotic, just like the opening quarter. After just a few minutes, Sandy signaled Keith to blow his whistle and conclude the game. We should've stopped at the end of the third quarter, Sandy thought to himself. Oh well, live and learn.

"Go get dressed," he told all the players, "and we'll meet for just a few minutes on the deck before you head home." While the parents milled about, Sandy busied himself with clean-up duties. He and Keith carried the two goals into the aquatic equipment room. Then he and the lifeguard on duty, Heather, put the lane ropes back into the pool, not an easy task. Sabrina collected and counted the caps. He was pleased that his girlfriend, Kristina, disassembled the small scorers table and homemade scoreboard and put them away.

One by one for the boys and two by two for the girls, the young players came back to the pool, having showered and dressed. They went to their parents, receiving hugs and words of encouragement. When it appeared that the entire group had returned, Sandy motioned everyone, parents and children alike, to gather around him. It continued to be noisy due to the crowd in the adjoining warm-water pool, but there was nowhere else to go as a birthday party was using the aquatic lobby. Raising his voice, Sandy spoke. "Thanks to all of you for coming today. I think we've made some substantial progress with our water polo program. I know it's hard to see with all the splashing that takes place in a game, both above the surface and below, but as the coach, I'm pleased. I know most of you want to get home in time to watch the Carolina-Duke basketball game, but I do have one more thing to do." Taking a small box from Sabrina, he opened it and held up a shiny medal. "I have engraved medals for all of today's polo players. They say 'Love Games Water Polo 2014.' With his sister's help, he handed them out, calling the names of the participating youngsters. "Clayton … Warner … Junior … Ben … Jose … Ellery … Janis … Savannah … Wanda … Princess … Nona … Lexie … Delia … here's one for Keith, my assistant coach … and again, thanks to all of you. Have a great weekend."

As the group left the pool, one of the dads looked over his shoulder and shouted at Sandy, "Who're you cheering for in today's game, Duke or Carolina?"

Sandy waved and smiled. "Actually, I'll be cheering for Western California when they take on Stanford later tonight."

Chapter Six

DOWN THE MOUNTAIN

It felt good to be back in action. At halftime, his teammate Keith Cartwright had turned to Sandy and asked, "How many goals do you have?" Gasping for air, Sandy replied, "Not enough. We're behind, 7-to-5. We've gotta pick it up in the third quarter."

The Masters team in Sandy's hometown was playing against a team located an hour's drive away. When he was asked to participate, he'd initially refused. "I haven't the time. I'm busy with my YMCA job and the kids' water polo program." Then he was informed that the neighboring community also had a beginning-level youth team and that they'd be willing to take on Sandy's team in a game following the Masters clash. After checking with his players and their parents and receiving approval, Sandy agreed: he'd play for the local Masters and then he'd coach his young 11- and 12-year-olds.

"It won't be easy," Sandy told those who would listen to him. "We've been playing five- or six-per-side in our small Downtown YMCA pool which is half shallow, half deep. When we go down the mountain to play on March 14th, we'll be competing seven-per-side in a larger, all-deep pool. It'll be an official game with two referees, a scoreboard, the works, including a crowd cheering for the host team. I hope our boys and girls are up to the challenge."

What he didn't tell anyone was that the opposing team was older, containing several 13- and 14-year-olds, and faster, with several of them being swift competitive swimmers. But it would be their first game, too, and he hoped they'd be as amateurish as his own group. He also contacted Hector, the local 14-year-old, and said, "We need you for this game, if you're available." To which Hector replied, "You can count on me."

When the day arrived, the Masters team departed from the Downtown YMCA in three vehicles. Sandy waved and said, "See you there," after which he and two of the parents of his young troupe piled into three other cars and, with 13 youngsters, headed down the mountain. With Sandy was his girlfriend Kristina, to whom he'd said, "I haven't played a game for quite awhile, so if I start drowning, you can jump in and rescue me." He added, "More seriously, I need you to keep the scorebook for our kids' team."

When they reached their destination and walked into the indoor pool, everyone stopped short and gazed in amazement. "Wow," declared Delia. "This pool is BIG!"

"Yeah," agreed Hector. "But there are a lot of pools like this scattered around. I've been to some of them with the Piranhas swim squad."

Sandy had seen dozens of such large-sized pools during his days in California. He'd played in them while at Golden Gate Community College and Western California University and at the U.S. training site in Los Alamitos. It took great swimming speed and stamina just to get up and down such pools, not to mention all the various water polo skills. When you added the body contact and occasional wrestling that was part of the game at its highest levels, it was easy to understand why the sport was ranked No. 1 in difficulty.

"Let's go into the locker rooms and get changed," Sandy instructed his team. "The boys can come with me, the girls can go with Kristina. Remember to lock your lockers. Bring your valuables into the pool with you, and we'll put everything into this big bag which Lexie's dad, Mr. Allyn, will keep in his possession. When we get back to the pool, sit with Kristina and Mr. Allyn and Mrs. Riley. I'll have to get in the water and warm-up and then play in the Masters game. You can watch and see how I do."

At halftime in the Masters game, those watching the contest would have to agree that Sandy was doing all right. And then some. The participants in the game, on both sides, were not bad. Mostly men in their 30s and 40s, supplemented by a few women, they had almost all played water polo somewhere during their college days. They knew the rules, and their skills were adequate. But they were no longer in top shape for playing a sport such as water polo. Practicing once or maybe twice weekly was the norm. Sandy's teammates had him playing the hole set position, which was not his usual spot, but at 6-3 and 220 pounds, the opposing team had no one who could stop him. When thrown the ball, he adroitly handled it with his right hand or his left hand, shrugged off the efforts of the man guarding him, rose high out of the water, and whipped a shot into the corner of the opposing cage. This happened twice. When the defender moved over to prevent him for scoring in this manner for a third time, Sandy pumped in a backhand shot from the opposite side. By halftime, he'd scored five times, but his team was still trailing by two goals.

"Can I make a suggestion?" he queried his teammates as they relaxed before starting the third stanza. They nodded their consent. "I'm betting they'll try to double-team me if I go back into the hole set position. So let's try something else." Pointing to a teammate, he said, "You usually play hole set, Pete, so you go there. You know what to do. I'll play back on defense and see if we can give our goalie, Charlie, a little help. He's done well in the first half, but we need to tighten up our defense in the second half if we hope to win. Be more aggressive. Make the refs call the fouls. Let's slow them down. Don't let 'em get off a good shot."

Sure enough, the host team placed two men back on hole defense, and when Pete saw he couldn't get free, he passed to Crystal, who was wide open on the side. She hesitated, took a few strokes forward, and then surprised everyone, herself included, by putting a left-handed shot into the cage. "Atta girl!" shouted Kristina from the sidelines. Sandy's team was guarding much closer when on defense, and midway through the period, one of the players was ejected, giving the opposing team an extra man. They took advantage of the situation and scored, again assuming a two-goal lead. But Pete retaliated for the club from the mountains, and as the quarter ended, it was 8-to-7. "Just one goal behind. Let's do more of the same in the fourth quarter. We can win this game," Sandy exhorted his teammates. "Let's get the ball into Pete and see if he can draw a foul."

It took several minutes of back and forth action before Pete received the ball in front of the opposing cage. He controlled the ball and turned his body as two defenders pounced on him, and as hoped for, the ref called a major foul. Now Sandy's team had an extra player. They passed the ball from one side to the other, seeking an opening, as the defending team concentrated on guarding Pete, in the hole, and Sandy, threatening from the outside. "Watch that big guy!" demanded the home coach from the deck, waving his hand toward Sandy. With two defenders crowding Pete and two more advancing toward Sandy, someone had to be open. Sandy spotted Keith Cartwright driving in from the left side. Keith stopped, used a hard egg-beater kick to rise up high, and received the pass thrown perfectly into his hand by Sandy. He rocketed a shot into the cage. The game was tied.

"Tough on defense!" Sandy reminded his teammates. "Don't give 'em a good shot." They responded to his command and gave up only a weak shot from the outside that goalie Charlie easily blocked. As soon as the shot was taken, Sandy sprinted from his defensive position down the pool. He hoped Charlie would see his move and get the ball to him. But Charlie passed to Keith on the other side. Darn, Sandy thought, but he kept on swimming hard, suddenly remembering that this was the way he'd taught his youngsters to do a fast break. One swimmer breaking down the side ... the goalie passing the ball to the other side ... and then the ball being tossed cross-pool to the breaking player. Maybe Keith, as his assistant, would also remember. Keith did. He placed a perfect pass in front of Sandy whose stroking arms controlled the ball, and as he approached the opposing cage, he did a quick pop-shot of the old-fashioned type that caught the goalie by surprise. The ball bounced off the goalie's shoulder and into the cage. Lucky shot, Sandy smiled, but I'll take it. The game ended a minute later with the visiting team from the mountains ahead, 9-to-8.

* * * * *

"You're famous," said Kristina, as she and Sandy enjoyed their usual Sunday afternoon stroll down the riverside path.

"Well, maybe semi-famous," Sandy conceded, with a smirk. The Citizen-Times newspaper had done a lengthy article about him and the YMCA's recently-rejuvenated water polo program. The article started by stating that Sandy had been a Y swimmer during his younger days and then had attended Golden Gate Community College and Western California University where he focused on water polo, becoming an All-American. He'd then spent nearly two years training at the national water polo venue in southern California before returning home. Now he was a member of the Downtown YMCA staff, serving as Head Lifeguard while also coaching a group of young poloists.

The article reported that "Sandy Scott led the local Masters squad to a surprise victory last weekend, scoring six goals in a 9-to-8 come-from-behind win. His length-of-the-pool dash and score with one minute to go sealed the verdict.

"More than that, Scott then coached the YMCA's young water poloists to an 8-to-5 triumph. This was the first official game for the local youth team since the 1970s, when the Y won a number of national championships, and 1984, when they hosted an Olympic Development Clinic."

Guiding Kristina to their favorite riverside bench, Sandy let his mind wander back to the second game played in the large pool at the nearby city on March 14th. After the Masters contest ended, he'd let Keith and Kristina put the Y's young players through their warm-up exercises. "Make sure they have a chance to shoot at the goals at both ends," he told them, "even if you have to disrupt what the home team is doing. Be pushy. Let's try to intimidate the opposing kids by letting them know that we're in charge of what's going on here. Oh," he added, "I see the home team still has the adult balls in the pool from the Masters game. Let's make sure they know enough to use the junior-size balls for the kids' competition. Just in case, I brought along a bag of 'em." He emptied the bag into the pool.

This pre-game strategy of attempting to upstage the home team seemed to work. Or maybe it was the fact that the home team's youngsters, while a bit older and bigger and maybe faster, weren't as adept at playing water polo as Sandy's young athletes.

When the game started, it became immediately evident that Sandy's squad knew how to play water polo while the home team kids didn't. Standing on the sidelines, Sandy said to Kristina and Keith, "I'll bet they've been doing almost all competitive swimming and have had only a couple of polo practices before today. Their passing is really bad, and they don't appear able to set up a strong offensive attack."

Sandy had started seven players who'd been in the program since the beginning and whom he thought would play well together. This included Jose as goalie and Ben as hole guard, with Ellery also helping out defensively, plus Princess, Junior, and Savannah in mid-pool, with Lexie as hole set. They'd never played seven-per-side in such a large pool, but Sandy crossed his fingers and hoped for the best. He didn't have to worry. The opposing team did a lot of swift but disorganized swimming and threw one inaccurate pass after another. When the passes were occasionally on-target, they were fumbled away by the receiver. It was a classic case of a swim team depending almost solely on its speed to succeed in the game of water polo. Didn't work. At least not often.

The contest remained scoreless until Sandy put 14-year-old Hector into action. He immediately captured the ball, dribbled downpool, stopped at the four-yard line, and powered a shot into the cage, beating the home team's goalie who was obviously inept. He did it again a minute later.

In the second period, Sandy put Delia into the game. She'd gradually been picking up the skills of the sport, and she could not only cover on defense but was also a threat offensively, at least against such a beginning-level opponent. In mid-quarter, she advanced into the offensive end of the pool, and when two opponents swam over to guard her, she passed to Lexie in the hole set spot, about three yards in front of the home team's goal. Given her first opportunity to score in the contest, Lexie demonstrated her unusual ability, elbowing the defender aside not only once but twice and then rising up high out of the water, turning, and blasting a shot into a corner of the cage.

At this point, Sandy's squad seemed to relax on defense. The host team took advantage and hit on a strong shot from the outside which skipped off Jose's fingers. Calling a timeout, Sandy gathered his gang in a circle and said, "There's just one minute to go before halftime. We have possession, so get the ball again to Lexie. If you can get off a good shot, Lexie, take it. If not, try to earn an ejection. Show the ref that you're being held, that you're being killed. If we get the ejection, let's set up three in the front row and three in the back row. We won't have much time, so I want you, Princess, or you, Ellery, to take the shot. Now don't be sloppy. Don't lose the ball. Okay, go for it!"

Advancing into the offensive end, the team did exactly as their coach had instructed. They passed the ball into Lexie, who put her hand on the ball and then removed it just as she was pummeled by the player guarding her. Lexie lifted both hands to show the referee that she was being fouled and looked pleadingly at the ref, who responded by blowing his whistle and ejecting the defensive player. "What a break," Sandy said to Kristina and Keith on the sidelines. "I never thought a hometown ref would make that call."

With a one-player advantage, the young visitors from the mountains quickly set it up, spreading themselves out. One pass was made, another, another, and Sandy, glancing at the scoreboard, saw that time was running out. "Shoot!" he shouted. And Princess did. It didn't take much to get the ball past the home team's goalie, and the ball settled into the cage as the horn sounded. At halftime, Sandy's squad was in front, 4-to-1.

"Now comes the test," Sandy said with a grimace, turning again to Kristina and Keith. "We have to play our subs in the third quarter. Can they keep the lead?"

"Do you have to put them in?" Keith asked.

"Yeah. You know the YMCA's philosophy. *At the Y, everyone plays.* Besides, they need the experience."

Sandy gathered his team members around him. "Listen up. The game isn't over yet. The other team is going to play better in the second half. You can count on it. Here's our lineup to start the third quarter. Hector, I want you back on defense, helping Nona, who'll be our goalie. Junior, you'll be up front as our hole set. You're our offense this quarter. If we can get the ball to you, take a shot. Their goalie isn't very good, so you should be able to score. In mid-pool, we'll have Warner and Wanda, Clayton, and Janis. Your job is to be tough on defense. Remember, this is *real* water polo, not Sandy

Ball. You don't need to keep your hands off the opposing players. Be aggressive. Grab. Push. Kick. Do whatever's necessary to harass the person you're guarding. You know what I told you at our last practice: they may be faster than we are, but how fast can they swim if you're holding on to them?" This brought a loud laugh from the group of youngsters. "Okay. Line up at the deep end. Be tough!"

His team was so aggressive, so tough, that Clayton immediately was called for a foul and ejected from the game for 30 seconds. "Oh, man," Sandy murmured. The home team had no idea what to do with the extra player, but Sandy's subs had no idea what to do on defense and gave up a score. Unable to make anything happen on offense, Sandy's squad relinquished the ball a minute later. Hector swam back and forth on defense, from one opponent to another, but to no avail. The home team scored again. It was now 4-to-3.

Sandy and Kristina exchanged glances. "Doesn't look good," she said.

"You're right," Sandy agreed. "Delia, hop in and help Hector on defense. Take Clayton's place."

With Clayton, the weakest player, out of the game, and Delia, a swift swimmer, helping out defensively, the situation improved. Hector even took a chance and dribbled into the offensive end. When guarded, he passed to Junior who, as Sandy predicted, was able to whip the ball past the home team's goalie.

At the brief break before the final five-minute period started, Sandy told his team, "The fourth quarter is ours. They've used their best players the entire game, and I'm sure they're getting tired. We had some of our players" – he was careful not to mention they were the best – "resting during the third quarter. So we'll be fresh. Nona, you stay in as goalie. Ben, you're our hole guard. Lexie, you're back in the game as our hole set. Let's have Ellery, Princess, Savannah, and Warner in mid-pool. We need to score a goal or two while being tough on defense in order to win this game. Don't be slack. Give it everything you've got."

By now the home team was starting to catch on to the intricacies of water polo. They were performing better. But Sandy's squad wasn't to be denied. They tasted victory. With Keith and Kristina and the two parents, Mr. Allyn and Mrs. Riley, shouting encouragement from the sidelines, the visitors from the mountains dribbled and passed well and, more importantly, were active on defense, battling every move made by the opposing players. The game blossomed into a more wide-open, up-and-down the pool contest, resembling to some small extent the way water polo was supposed to be played. The teams traded goals. Princess scored. The home team scored. Sandy said, "Delia, you go in for Ellery. Get the ball to Lexie." She did, and Lexie scored. The home team tallied once more. "Wanda, you go in for Warner, your brother, and Janis, you go in for Ben. Be tough on defense." With less than two minutes remaining and his team trailing by two goals, the home team coach finally inserted a trio of subs, who were young and not only slow but also absolute beginners. "Bring it home!" Sandy shouted, and Delia splashed past the pokey opponents. This time, instead of passing to Lexie as she'd done previously, she stopped at the four-yard line, executed a strong egg-beater kick, reared back, and fired a bullet into the cage. That's how it ended, with the score favoring Sandy's squad, 8-to-5.

Now, as Sandy sat on the riverside bench and recalled how the kids' game had unfolded, he was poked in the ribs by Kristina, who interrupted his reverie. "Hello, hot-shot, what're you dreaming about?"

"Oh, I was thinking about the game. After it ended, the coach of the opposing team came to me and said how rough our kids played. I was happy to hear it. I told him we weren't in a swimming meet but rather in a water polo match. Big difference."

* * * * *

After the article appeared in the newspaper about the YMCA's youth water polo team winning its game, the Y received a dozen inquiries from families who wanted to join Sandy's program. "We don't have room for any more right now," he told Tina and Lydia. "Let's put them on a waiting list, and maybe we can enroll them this summer."

The team was still practicing in the Downtown YMCA's lap pool on Tuesdays and Thursdays from 5:00 to 6:00. But they'd relinquished usage of lane four on Friday afternoons. It hadn't worked out, and furthermore, Sandy needed that slot for the springtime junior lifesaving course he was conducting. On a more positive note, he'd arranged for his team to use the local college pool on Saturday mornings from 9:30 to 11:00. "I know it's not convenient for you," he told the parents, and "I know you'd like to sleep late on Saturdays," he told the kids, "but we have to take what we can get." The college pool was large, deep, and had makeshift goals that were used for the school's intramural inner-tube water polo league. Best of all, the college swim coach had given them the pool for 10 weeks, free of charge. She said, "You're a non-profit serving our community, and we're a public university serving our community, and there's no reason we can't work together." Sandy suspected she also hoped that some of the YMCA's fast competitive swimmers might be enticed into joining her college team in the near future if she demonstrated her willingness to cooperate with the Y.

He thought he'd done a decent job of planning for March, April, and May, but when he detected some grumbling from behind the scenes, he decided to call another meeting of the parents. He also decided to again contact the former coach and pick his brain. He'd spoken previously with the ol' coach on the phone. Now he requested they meet for lunch. Sitting there in a booth, Sandy was a bit anxious. He expected the 81-year-old man to limp into the restaurant, perhaps using a cane, with white hair and a physique that was showing its age. Instead, he was approached by a gentleman who, despite his age, was standing tall and appeared to be quite healthy. "Hey, Coach, thanks for coming," he said. "You look great."

"It's a privilege for me to meet you," the man replied. "You can call me Champ, if you don't mind. For some reason, that's what my water polo players named me many moons ago, and the name has stuck."

"I'm not surprised. You were a great athlete and a champion coach."

"Not at all. I was an average athlete in several sports – swimming, kayaking, water polo – and an ordinary coach whose outstanding players made me look good."

"Well, Coach ... I mean Champ ... I know better than that. Let's order, and then I have a few questions to ask you." When the waitress arrived, Sandy ordered the salmon, while the ol' coach ordered a club sandwich. "With iced tea," he added, and then, looking across the table, he said, "You are I have a lot in common, Sandy. I learned to play water polo in the Midwest before coming here. You learned to play out in California before returning home. We both loved the game so much that we wanted to teach the kids here. It wasn't easy for me, and I know it's not been easy for you."

Sandy nodded his head. "You're right. My paying job is with the YMCA. I'm the Head Lifeguard. I do the water polo on the side."

"Same with me," Champ stated. "People tend to forget that I was hired as the YMCA's Director of Aquatics. I did it all in those days ... operating the lap pool which opened in 1970, with the warm-water therapy pool added in 1986 ... doing the pool maintenance which included backwashing and vacuuming every weekend ... teaching the swimming and kayaking courses and occasionally the other classes such as skin-diving ... lifeguarding myself and directing the lifeguard staff. Like you, Sandy, I always felt that safety came first, and I'm pleased to say that during my 20 years of aquatic supervision, we never had a serious injury."

"When did you find time for water polo?"

"I coached both the junior swim team and the water polo teams at the Downtown YMCA. We fit it into the pool schedule, altogether about 10 hours weekly. That's for the junior swimmers and the boys' and girls' water polo teams combined. It wasn't enough practice time, even in those days, so we found additional time for water polo at various other pools. My boss, a good guy, said that was all right with him so long as I did the coaching at the other pools on my own time and didn't count it as 'Y time.' I normally worked 44 hours at the YMCA each week and devoted another 10 hours of 'my time' to coaching and promoting water polo. No regrets. I'd do it all again."

"So you coached competitive swimming, too?"

"Yes. I started out as a swimmer myself before transferring to water polo in my 20s. I think swimming, as an individual sport, teaches young children to take responsibility for their actions. Generally, they sink or swim, win or lose, on their own. Water polo, meanwhile, teaches them to use their skills not only for themselves but for others, as well. It's a good educational combination.

"We had a junior swim team of about 30 pre-teens at the Downtown YMCA. Didn't have much practice time, but we did all right. It was mostly dual meets in those days, competing against other Ys. To repeat myself, I saw swimming as being a stepping-stone for water polo. Almost all of our young swimmers moved on to water polo as teens, but they continued to represent us in the dual swim meets during the indoor season. We had an 80-8-1 record in swimming. Not bad."

Champ paused, caught his breath, and continued, "If a youngster didn't want to play polo, I suggested they find another activity. There was a strong AAU swim squad in town, and some of our Y swimmers went there. For those remaining at the Y, we offered junior lifesaving, kayaking, skin-diving, and the leaders club. But most of the young swimmers in our program thoroughly enjoyed playing water polo. I remember that one year we had 41 teen girls and 22 teen boys signed up for the sport. I didn't know where to put them all."

"I might be facing the same problem," Sandy said. "What did you do?"

"We used two other indoor pools in town, and in the summer we used two more outdoor pools. On occasion, we ended up shooting at benches placed at both ends of the pools. It was hectic, but somehow we made it work."

With their lunches having arrived, the two men busied themselves with eating. Eventually Sandy asked, "What did you do for water polo competition?"

"In that respect," the ol' coach answered, "we had it better than you do. Water polo was a sanctioned YMCA sport in the 1960s and 1970s, so a lot of Ys were fielding teams. We played Greenville, Greensboro, High Point, Spartanburg, Shelby, and Raleigh from here in the Carolinas, plus other Y teams from Georgia, Kentucky, and Tennessee. Our boys took on the best Y teams from around the East and Midwest." He took a bite of his sandwich and said, "Our boys also played 10 or so college men's teams in their campus pools. That was tough, but I recall our beating Duke, Vandy, Virginia, Western Carolina, and one or two others. Not bad."

"What about your girls?" Sandy wondered.

"Ah, that was a different era. When we began here, Title IX hadn't been passed by Congress. There were very few opportunities for women and girls in sports. I'd been elected chairman of the AAU's national women's water polo committee in 1965 and continued to serve in that position year after year, mainly because no one else wanted to do it. I'd coached Y girls' swimming and water polo in the Midwest, dating back to the 1950s for swimming and early 1960s for polo. I enjoyed it. So I was enthused about continuing after I arrived here in August of 1969. We began with about 10 girls and practiced just once or perhaps twice weekly. We won half-a-dozen games against the other beginning-level teams in this area. Then we decided to attend the Junior Olympic Championships in St. Louis. We got blasted by teams that were better. Lost three games, tied one, and finished last. I felt this would put a damper on my efforts with the local girls, but it didn't. They kept on coming to our practices, more and more and more of them. I kept on coaching, the parents kept on paying the dues and fees and travel costs, and we ended up winning a number of national water polo titles, including the JOs, and representing the U.S. internationally. It was quite something."

Sandy was curious. "So, Champ, you weren't playing coed polo in those days?"

"Not in the 1970s. The boys and girls practiced separately and once weekly would come together to scrimmage. They were very supportive of each other. We finally started playing coed water polo in the 1980s and kept at it in the 1990s. Never had any problems."

"Your girls traveled a lot, didn't they?"

"Sure did. We had to. While the boys found good competition in this area from other Ys and a few AAU clubs and, of course, the colleges they played, our girls had to travel extensively to find the competition they needed. I had our girls divided into varsity, junior varsity, and 'C' teams, and they all took major trips. The varsity flew to tourneys in Albuquerque, Omaha, Miami, Fresno, Honolulu, and finally to Montreal and Quebec City for the World Club Championships. The JVs flew to Miami and Philly. Even the 'C' team, the beginners, flew to Albuquerque and Miami. I wanted each group to play nationally and, in the process, have a good educational experience."

"But," observed Sandy wryly, "you must have favored sunny south Florida with each team traveling to Miami."

"From a personal standpoint, I've loved south Florida since I first went there as a 19-year-old. I've taken many trips there over the years, primarily to Fort Lauderdale and Miami, and my wife Lee and I, as avid skin-divers, vacationed often in the Florida Keys. When our daughter Heather grew older, we took her with us. We even thought about retiring in the Keys at one time. From a water polo standpoint, Miami had the best women's teams in the country in the late 1960s and throughout the 1970s. So we played down there on three occasions, and their teams came here three or four times to compete in the tourneys that we hosted at the college pool. We met in other events around the country. At first, they socked it to us. They were bigger and better. Eventually we caught up with 'em as our varsity girls continued playing together for six or seven years. We had really, really good teamwork by then."

The ol' coach hesitated a moment, collecting his thoughts, and then said, "I guess I'm most proud of the fact that our girls beat the top four California women's teams at one time or another, either in their pools or in neutral pools. We also whipped the University of Hawaii women's team in their pool. For a group of teenaged girls from the remote mountains of Western North Carolina to do this was almost unbelievable." He sighed and settled back in his seat. "Sorry to talk so much."

"No, no," Sandy waved him off. "I'm happy to hear about your efforts in the past. Now that we've finished eating, I have to get back to work, but I have one or two final questions."

"Fire away," Champ said.

"How could you and your girls afford to go on such long trips? It must have been expensive."

"Actually, we took just one long plane trip each year which, divided up between the varsity, JVs, and 'C' team, was usually manageable for the families. I always paid my own way, which I think set a good example and which the parents of the kids appreciated. We did a lot of sight-seeing and promoted each trip as an educational adventure. Also, after the first two years, we started winning nationally and producing All-Americans, and everyone jumped on our band-wagon, so we received some community support. Finally, we conducted frequent fund-raising activities so the girls could raise at least a part of the costs for themselves. We did a swim-a-thon each year. We had car washes and bake sales. We held dances in the Downtown YMCA gym for which we charged a small amount. You know, the usual stuff. Still, there were times when we had to leave a player or two behind because, well, the family just couldn't afford it at the time. Unfortunately, that's life."

"Well," Sandy was prompted to say, "your players were older than mine are at present, so they had more options, I suppose."

"Hmmm. Perhaps. But youngsters mature more rapidly nowadays, particularly the girls. I suspect your 11- and 12-year-olds are as mature physically as the 13- and 14-year-old girls with whom I worked 40 years ago. I've been watching some of the present-day 11- and 12-year-old teams from California on videos, and whoa, they can play polo! So don't back off, Sandy. If you challenge your youngsters to keep on improving and put them up against the toughest opponents you can find, they'll surprise you. I guarantee it."

* * * * *

It was a Saturday morning during spring vacation, and Sandy's squad had just completed a 90-minute workout at the college pool. The first hour had been devoted to swimming. "We've spent the last six or seven months learning the basics of water polo," he told the kids, "and you can now do the egg-beater kick which lifts you up out of the water. This is a vital skill in the sport. You can pass and catch the ball reasonably well. Your shooting is not great, but it's all right. You've been able to move from Sandy Ball, our hands-up version of the game, to the more aggressive form of water polo and, in fact, your guarding has become excellent. I love it. It was our defensive work, the guarding you did and the goaltending by Jose and Nona, that enabled us to win the game last month. We shut down a team that was faster than we were. But they were beginners. When we play opponents that are fast and know how to play the game, which'll happen if we go to Philadelphia, we'll be in trouble. So whether you like it or not, we have to work on swimming speed and stamina. That'll be our focus this month and next."

Philadelphia. Really, Sandy thought to himself? Would it happen? After meeting with the ol' coach, he'd scheduled a meeting with the parents. They were enthused about the team's on-the-road triumph but inquisitive about what the future might bring. Several were somewhat dismayed that the cost of the program had increased. "Look," Sandy told them, "I'm doing everything I can to keep the costs down. I'm not getting paid to coach, nor is Keith, who's helping out as my assistant. I've arranged to use the college pool on Saturdays free of charge. We're scrimping along with a minimum of equipment. We've only taken one trip, and it was just down the mountain and then back home in a single day. What else can I do?" Sandy knew that the YMCA also had reduced the membership fees for several of his water polo families, but he didn't want to mention that in front of the entire group of parents.

"We're with you, Sandy," spoke up the mother of twins Warner and Wanda. "We just need clarification of what you're planning for the immediate future."

"As I mentioned when we met two months ago, there's a tournament in Philadelphia in May for 12-and-unders. I said it was my dream for us to enter. So whatd'ya think? Is it a possibility? The teams there are topnotch, and we'd probably get our butts kicked, if you'll pardon my language. But if you're interested in my pursuing the idea, I'll see if I can arrange for our kids to stay in the homes of one of the Philly teams, which'll cut down costs considerably, and I'll try and set up a sight-seeing itinerary. It'd be a great educational adventure for your sons and daughters."

"Would you fly or drive?" asked Mrs. Riley.

"You tell me. Go home and talk it over, all of you, and let me know what you think."

Now, standing outside the college pool at the conclusion of the Saturday morning practice, Sandy watched as the same parents with whom he'd been talking at the recent meeting arrived in their cars and picked up the young water poloists. They waved at Sandy, and he waved back. Well, he thought, they're doing their share. God bless the moms and dads. They get the kids to our practices, and they pay the costs to the best of their ability, and it appears they're going to give me the green light to take the team to Philly. I only hope I'm worthy of their trust.

CHAPTER SEVEN

PURPOSEFUL PLANNING

"So how's your secret plan working?" Sabrina asked her older brother as the family gathered around the dinner table. "I remember you telling us a month or so ago that you had a plan for recruiting a few more players."

"Not so good," Sandy replied. "My plan was to teach water polo to the home school group that uses the Y pools once weekly. They have about 20 kids from elementary to high school who attend. I hoped I'd find two or three prospects."

"And?" his dad inquired.

"Actually, they've enjoyed the water polo I've taught them. In the past, they either had swim lessons or play time, so they were ready for something new and exciting."

"What happened?"

"Apparently there's a home school sports league that offers soccer, basketball, softball, and the like. They compete amongst themselves and against home schoolers from other towns. Almost all the kids who come to the Y to swim are participating in the league. They say they just don't have time for three water polo practices each week. I guess I have to admit that my plan hasn't worked out. On the other hand ..."

"Yes?" his normally quiet grandmother spoke up. "Now, Sandy, eat your salad," she said, "and tell us more."

"Two new players from the Y's autumn and winter swim classes have joined the team. Both have passed their advanced tests which included performing a timed quarter-mile swim. They're just beginners at water polo, of course, but I'm happy to have them."

"Will they be ready for the trip to Philadelphia?"

"No, and I'm still working on the trip. I've ended up telling the parents that the decision is up to them. The parents of the best players are all for it. The parents of the not-so-good, the subs, remain hesitant. Right now, altogether, we have seven who say yes, two who say no, with four still undecided. The cost may be the determining factor for them. I'm going to take a chance and contact the polo people in Philly and ask about our entering their May tournament. Cross your fingers that they say yes and that we can then come up with a full team."

Mr. Scott smiled. "You've always had a positive attitude, Sandy. I admire it."

"Hey, you taught me well, dad. Nothing ventured, nothing gained."

Mrs. Scott intruded on the male egos. "Don't forget there's another saying. It goes like this: the best laid plans of mice and men oft go awry."

"Yeah," Sandy admitted, "that, too."

"That's enough philosophizing," interjected his grandfather. "I'm ready for a second helping. Pass the spaghetti, please."

* * * *

It was Sabrina's turn to grab the spotlight. The YMCA's swim team, the Piranhas, had qualified 10 swimmers for the National Short Course Championships, and one was Sabrina. She wasn't the star and hadn't even made it in any individual events, but she was part of the qualifying 400-yard medley relay quartet. The Scott family followed the meet closely on the internet, with reports being sent home by Coaches Kirk, Kiki, and Chris. "Our medley relay unit, all underclassmen, er, women," Chris commented, "reached the consolation finals. I believe they could win it all within the next year or two. As you know, one of the relay girls won her individual event, the breaststroke, and our best boy placed third in the IM. You can be proud of ALL our swimmers!"

Sandy remembered his two trips to the YMCA Nationals, held at Fort Lauderdale, Florida. He'd been fairly fast in his races and had once reached the consolation finals. He and his teammates had toured the International Swimming Hall of Fame and also enjoyed splashing in the ocean waves. He could understand why Champ, the former Y coach, liked south Florida so much.

But that was then, and this is now, he reminded himself as he walked into the Downtown YMCA's aquatic office for a meeting with staff members Tina and Lydia. After a few minutes of easy chit-chat, they got down to business. "Yes," Sandy said, "we DID have a problem recently with one of our lifeguards. He wasn't paying attention, and two of our older swimmers collided in mid-pool while sharing a lane. One was injured, slightly. I know he complained to you, Lydia, but he was back in the water two days later. It happened so quickly I'm not sure what the lifeguard could have done. Nonetheless I've talked with him about being more alert. We haven't had to make any rescues for the past two months. Shows that we're doing a good job of preventive lifeguarding."

"How's your training for the guards going?" Lydia asked.

"All 12 have been doing their fitness swims as scheduled. So have I. The Y branch on the South side of town is conducting a senior lifesaving class this spring, so I'm not duplicating their efforts. I'm running a junior lifesaving course on Friday afternoons, as you know. We have just seven enrolled, fewer than I expected, but it's a good group."

"Okay," Tina intervened. "That's a helpful report, Sandy. I assume your kids' water polo program is continuing to show progress."

"I think it is. We're still practicing here at the Y for an hour on the late afternoons of each Tuesday and Thursday, and I've added a Saturday morning practice at the college pool. When we changed from Sandy Ball to bona fide water polo, we lost several kids, but we still have 12 from the original group, and we've added one who's transferred from the Piranhas and two more from the Y's autumn and winter advanced swim classes. I'm told that after the newspaper article, about a dozen families from around the community called and asked about having their youngsters join the program. We've put them off until this summer when, hopefully, I'll have more pool time. Right now I have all I can handle as a coach, a *volunteer* coach, especially with the trip to Philadelphia looming in a few weeks."

"How's it look for the Philly trip?"

"I'm working on it, both here with our families and there with the people who're running the 12-and-under tournament."

"Do you have the YMCA's permission to go? You'll be representing the Y, you know."

"Gosh, I hadn't thought about it."

"Well, if you go, there's some paperwork that needs to be done," Tina declared. "I can do that for you, but please don't wait until the last minute. I'm plenty busy myself supervising a spring basketball league for adults and youth programming in field hockey, lacrosse, soccer, and T-ball. I'm already working on summer rugby and our autumn Pop Warner football program."

"Never a dull moment at the Y, you know," Lydia lamented, "but we all love it, right?"

The meeting ended soon thereafter, and Sandy strolled into the two-pool Aquatic Center. Sitting on a bench along the deck of the lap pool, he watched the swimmers as they splashed from one end to the other. He waved at the two lifeguards who were working, but because the lap pool and the adjoining warm-water therapy pool were full, he didn't want to distract the guards from their duties. Both, he noted, were properly clad and carrying their rescue tubes and keeping a close eye on the swimmers. He didn't have anything scheduled for the remainder of the day, so he began pondering – what else? – his youth water polo program. With no one else apparently noticing, he'd concluded the recent game against the team from down the mountain with a lineup of ALL GIRLS. As the fourth quarter reached its halfway mark, he'd had Lexie, Delia, Savannah, Princess, Nona, Janis, and Wanda in the water. Five of the girls were 12-year-olds, several of them just having turned that age, and they were coming along nicely. Lexie, the willowy one, remained the best of the bunch. She was a decent swimmer and, more importantly, played the hole set spot with amazing skill for one so young. She battled for position in front of the opposing goal, wasn't scared to mix it up with whoever tried to defend her, and had a strong shot. She could have been a star at basketball or soccer or some other sport, but she seemed to prefer water polo. Thankfully, Sandy acknowledged, with a smile.

Nona was developing into a respectable goalie. She was a little on the short side and had difficulty reaching the corners of the

10-foot-wide by three-foot-high cage, but she had quick hands and didn't duck when the ball was thrown directly at her. She still wasn't much of a swimmer and disappeared into the locker room when Sandy had the team doing a series of sprints, but he looked the other way and didn't chastise her. Princess, with her sturdy body, swam well and was always eager to shoot and score. She had a good shot. However, she tended to loaf on defense. Savannah was just the opposite. She was developing into an excellent defender and passed reasonably well, but she was hesitant to take a shot. The fifth 12-year-old was Delia, who'd transferred from the Piranhas swim squad. She gave them some real speed at mid-pool and was gradually picking up the finer points of the game.

The two 11-year-olds, Wanda and Janis, had a ways to go. They weren't yet very good at anything – dribbling, passing, shooting, guarding – but they were learning. The newest girl, Cindy, who'd just completed the Y's advanced swim class and joined the team, also was 11. She swam well and seemed willing to do the dribbling, passing, and catching at practice, but she was shy and non-aggressive, and the first time she joined in a scrimmage session, she'd backed away from the action. Well, Sandy thought, that'll change. Hopefully. We DO have the ingredients for a good girls' team, the young coach concluded.

As for the boys, it was too early to predict. They needed another year or two before beginning to mature physically. It was Hector, at the age of 14, who currently kept the boys together. When he was playing, they did all right. When he was absent, the 11- and 12-year-olds floundered. They did the best they could – Ellery, Ben, Junior, Warner, little Clayton, goalie Jose, and the newcomer from the YMCA swim classes, Leland – and if they kept at it, they might become big and strong and proficient poloists. Only time would tell.

So why am I sitting here all by my lonesome, Sandy asked himself? If I haven't anything else to do, I can always swim. He stood, stretched, and headed for the locker room to change into his swim suit. Hey, the water will feel great, as usual.

* * * * *

"Let's go somewhere else," Kristina suggested after church on Sunday. "The riverside park is nice, but I'd like to go to … how about the Nature Center?" Sandy nodded, saying, "Okay, you should fit right in."

"What do you mean?"

"That you're one foxy young lady."

"Hmmm. Should I take that as a compliment?" Kristina raised her eye brows.

"I hope so. I think of someone who's foxy as being both cute and, ah, cunning."

"I'll accept the cute part as being well-meaning. Not sure about the cunning part, though. With what animal do you identify, Sandy?"

"Do I have to pick just one?" he answered, maneuvering his car into the right-hand lane on the cross-town expressway.

"Yes. Are you not familiar with such concepts as avatars, otherkin, and totems? What did you study in college, anyway?"

"I earned a degree in Recreation Administration. Took the usual courses along the way. Why? What did I miss?"

Kristina shook her head. "If you're going to work with today's youngsters and relate to them, you must connect with the virtual world. It's somewhat similar to the spirit world in that it exists beyond the ordinary. You can't see it, but you can feel it. You know it's there. Not only in your computer but all around you."

"Like a fourth dimension?"

"Sort of. The fourth dimension probably exists in the *real* world of physics. We as a species just haven't found it yet. The virtual world is more meta-physical, or beyond our reach. But it's there. Hey, how did we get on this subject? Let me return to my original question: with what animal do you identify, Sandy?"

The strong, strappling young man turned into the parking lot at the city's Nature Center, a fancy name for the local zoo. "I've always felt somewhat related to the river otters. What do you think of that?"

"They have otters here. Let's take a look at them, and I'll let you know."

After parking in the one space left open on a busy Sunday afternoon and paying the admission fee, Sandy and Kristina walked hand in hand through the Nature Center. It was packed with families enjoying a sunny spring day. They passed by cages and areas that housed bears and bobcats, mammals and reptiles, coyotes ands wolves and, yes, foxes. They stopped at the bird sanctuary and tried to identify the wide variety of flying creatures. Walking onward, Kristina pointed ahead. "There it is. Otter Falls." They jostled their way into the viewing area and watched half-a-dozen of the sleek, furry two-to- three-foot-long animals cavorting in the water, sliding down the slanted logs, and nudging each other. It was quite a performance.

"Did you know," Kristina said, "that otters have an extra eyelid? When they're underwater, it closes over their eyes to provide protection, but it's transparent so they can see through it."

"Wow. Wouldn't it be wonderful if we humans had something similar? We wouldn't have to bother with goggles."

"Who knows what the future will bring? Humankind may be living entirely underwater on this planet and on other planets, as well. We may be visiting other galaxies, maybe even other universes. Or we may all be living in different realities, moving from one dimension to another. It's possible, you know. We'll most likely be interacting with other forms of life, other sentient species. Humanity in the year 3000 will certainly be a lot different from what we're experiencing now, in the year 2014." Kristina led Sandy to a bench and continued. "Let's take a break and rest awhile."

They sat in silence for several minutes, watching the hundreds of visitors to the Nature Center, young and older, flocking past them. Finally Sandy said, "Moving from the year 3000 back here to the present, how're your studies coming, Kristina?"

"I'm doing okay. As you know, I concluded my Nurse Assistant program a year ago and then passed the state exam, so I'm a CNA. That's a Certified Nurse Assistant. Unfortunately, the only jobs available around here nowadays are menial and pay barely above the minimum wage. Hard work, long hours, low pay. If I weren't still living at home, I couldn't make it."

"Yeah," Sandy stated emphatically. "Same with me, and I have a college degree."

"Anyway, I'm continuing with my courses at the community college. Should earn a two-year Associates degree in a few months and then maybe, hopefully, someday I'll become a Registered Nurse. That's my goal. The lifeguarding job at the Y enables me to pay for my college tuition and books, and keep my car running. But you already know that. What're your plans?"

"I promised the Y that I'd be the Head Lifeguard for a year, and I'm two-thirds of the way through my commitment. They've given me a free hand in developing the youth water polo program, which is great, although we could use more practice time. Generally I enjoy what I'm doing, and because, like you, I'm back to living at home, my expenses are relatively low. However, I can't say that I willingly tell everyone that I, a 25-year-old college grad, am going to sleep each night in my childhood bed."

"Is it comfortable?"

"Sure is."

"So you can't complain, can you? Plus I know your mom is feeding you well." Kristina stood and reached down to grasp Sandy's hand, pulling him up from the bench. "Let's head out, Otter man. I want to hear how your trip to Philadelphia is coming."

As they walked back to the parked car, Sandy smiled and said, "I haven't mentioned the best part of my life nowadays."

"What's that?"

"It's you, of course."

"Are you glad you didn't stay in California?"

"I liked it there and met a lot of cool people. I learned to play water polo the right way. But if I had to choose between staying out there and making the national team or being back home with you, I know which I'd select."

"Which is? No, don't tell me. I want to hear about the trip to Philly."

Opening Kristina's car door and letting her slide in, Sandy waited until he was seated himself and started the ignition before replying. "I've been in touch with the polo people there. They have a May tournament for 12-and-unders. It's sponsored by American Water Polo, which is headquartered in a Philly suburb. There are two divisions, one for kids who're experienced and one for kids who're relative beginners, which is where we'd be placed. Most of the teams are from the Philadelphia area, where water polo is a major sport with age group, high school, collegiate, and Masters competition. But they've had teams participating in the tourney from two or three other states. When I spoke with someone at American Water Polo, he informed me the organization is trying to expand its efforts nationwide. When I asked him about the possibility of a team of youngsters entering from Western North Carolina. he said he didn't see why not. So I'm hopeful."

"Well, Coach of Sandy Ball, time is running short. It's now mid-April."

"Shhhhh. Don't tell anyone, and I mean ANYONE, but I've already booked airline tickets for 12 of us from Asheville through Charlotte to Philly and back again on the weekend of the tourney. That's for two adults and 10 kids. I put it on my credit card."

"Oh, Sandy, are you sure you know what you're doing?"

"Time will tell, my sweet. Now, if you don't mind, I'd like to swing past the Downtown YMCA and make sure our Sunday afternoon lifeguards are performing their jobs in a professional manner."

"Can't you ever take a break?"

"You know what you said about being a CNA. Hard work, long hours, low pay. Same with those of us who work for the YMCA."

* * * * *

Given their choice, the water polo boys elected to have an overnight camp-out rather than attending a game being played by the city's minor league baseball team. The girls decided to have a sleep-over at one of the homes. It was part of Sandy's "team building" plan. He and his assistant, Keith, would accompany the boys. His sister, Sabrina, and girlfriend, Kristina, would chaperone the girls. When it was over, Sandy could only look back with some degree of dismay at what had happened. A severe spring rainstorm had spoiled the camp-out. Reporting to his parents as he so often did, he said, "We were gathered around the fire when the storm hit. Not only rain, but hail. Then came the wind. We rushed into the one big tent we had and … well, you get the picture … half-a-dozen young boys huddled together and shaking and shivering while Keith and I tried to console them. We eventually tried to catch a few winks in our sleeping bags, but rain kept creeping into the tent, and then the boys, one after another, had to go outside to go to the bathroom, which was a designated spot in the woods. You can imagine what a parade that looked like. By the time we returned home the next morning, we were all as wet as if we'd spent the night practicing in the Y pools." He paused and then added, "But you know what? I bet that 30 years from now, the boys will remember the night as being a big adventure and a lot of fun."

Sabrina told the tale of the sleep-over. "You know how it goes with young girls. Loud music, jumping on the beds, pillow fights, sharing secrets, talking about boys, texting friends, and all the rest. Then, as Sandy knows by now, in the middle of the night, Lexie gets up to go to the bathroom and, walking down a dark hallway, she trips over a toy left there and falls, injuring her wrist. At first we thought it might be broken. But when her parents took her to the doc the next morning, he said it was only sprained. Unfortunately, it's her shooting hand and will take at least two weeks to heal properly."

"Yeah," Sandy muttered. "I remember what Mom said. Something about the best-laid plans of mice and men oft going awry." Then, trying to see the bright side, as was his custom, Sandy said, "The doc put a waterproof cast on her wrist and said she can get in the pool, but she can't use her right hand for passing, catching, or shooting until he gives his approval. He figures two weeks. It may take one more week for her to regain her shooting skills. That's right when we'll be heading to Philly, so hopefully she'll be back to normal by then. In the meantime, I can tell the other players that they'll have to pick up their scoring efforts, which is something they need to do, anyway."

Arriving at the YMCA the following morning, he was approached by Lydia, the Director of Aquatics. "What's this I hear about your star player?"

Sandy told her the sad story. "But," he concluded, "she should be ready for the trip to Philadelphia. I hope so, or we'll be in big trouble."

"So you're really taking the team to Philly?"

"Looks like it. The polo people there have given us permission to enter, and I'm hoping our kids can stay in the homes of the kids from the hosting team. That'll save us money. Your compatriot on the Y staff, Tina, the Director of Sports, is doing the paperwork and is even asking the board of directors to pay the entry fee for us. I've bought airline tickets for 12 of us."

"Wow. You've done a lot of purposeful planning, Sandy. How'd you pay for the plane tickets?"

"I put 'em on my credit card."

"Isn't that taking a chance? How much was it?"

"Let's see. That's 12 of us times $350 apiece. Adds up to a bit over $4,000. Of course, I'm hoping the families of the participating players will all reimburse me. So far we have seven or eight who're committed to what I'm calling an educational adventure. Visiting with kids and their families in another state should be educational, don't you think, and I'm also arranging for our gang to take a bus tour of downtown Philadelphia and see the historical sites."

At practice the next day, the youngsters were both delighted and dejected. The joy came from realizing that the long-anticipated trip to Philadelphia was becoming a reality. Furthermore, they'd be flying! Only two had ever been on a plane. The downside resulted from Lexie's absence. She hadn't shown up. It was the first practice she'd missed since the program started eight months previously. Sandy forced himself to concentrate on making it a serious session without her.

The 12 in attendance did a quarter-mile of easy swimming to loosen the muscles. Then they did a variety of passing drills. This was followed by taking shots after receiving dry passes. "Catch and shoot, all in one motion," Sandy shouted. For older athletes, a pump and fake move was useful, but for these 11- and 12-year-olds, the coach kept it simple. "Just aim for the corners." Next came dribbling sprints. "Go, go, go. Elbows up. Kick. Harder." Then he had a defensive player chase the dribbler downpool and try to steal the ball. "Reach under," he instructed. "You know that. Reach under the dribbler's arms."

His players were becoming exhausted, so he gathered them in the usual corner at the shallow end of the pool. He hopped in himself and stood looking down at their eager faces. Speaking over the noise created by the family swim in the adjoining warm-water therapy pool, he said, "You're lookin' good today. I hope the boys' camp-out and the girls' sleep-over this past weekend rekindled your enthusiasm. Both groups had a few problems" – he laughed, and the kids joined in the laughter – "yet here we are, having fun in the pool once again. But it's serious fun. It's fun with a purpose. It's not play time. Next week I'll bring you and your parents up to date on the trip to Philly. Now I'll only say that you'll be playing seven-per-side in a big pool and that the teams you'll be playing are darn good. But you're getting good yourselves. I think we can hold our own."

Someone in the group murmured something and Sandy heard the comment. "You're asking if we'll have a chance without Lexie. Well, I believe Lexie's wrist will be healed by then and she'll be making the trip. That's what her doctor is predicting. Even if she doesn't go, we'll manage. We do, however, have to prepare for every occasion. Junior has done well playing the hole set spot for the boys. But if Lexie isn't available, now or at some time in the future, we need to find one of the girls to replace her as the hole set. I'd like to try Savannah today and Wanda on Thursday. What's that, Princess? You want to try hole set, too? Well, maybe, but I think we need to have you shooting from the outside. You have the strongest arm on the team, of all the girls. That's pretty important. So we'll see. Now let's go down to the deep end and set up. I want you in the hole position right now, Savannah, about two or three yards in front of the goal. We'll take turns passing the ball to you ..."

The practice continued for another 20 minutes before it was time to quit. As usual, the goals at each end had to be removed and stored in the aquatic equipment room, the lane ropes reinserted into the pool, the caps collected and counted, and the half-dozen balls dumped into the big ball bag. As the team members completed these chores and headed to the locker rooms to shower and dress, Sandy checked his clip board to see if he'd written any notes to himself. He'd written one. It said, "Savannah can do this ... play hole set if necessary ... but we need to replace her in mid-pool. With whom?"

Sitting on the bench that ran the length of the lap pool, he answered his own question. How about Beatrice? She'd dropped out of water polo but had enrolled in the spring junior lifesaving course, which he was teaching. She was doing well and was still in shape. Maybe he could entice her back into the polo program with the prospect of an exciting trip to Philadelphia. Her parents could afford it. Hey, where there's a will, there's a way.

Chapter Eight

PHILLY FUN AND GAMES

"Clip your nails, especially you girls," Sandy reminded his team as they gathered on the deck of the college pool. "And make sure your hair is short enough to be tucked into the water polo caps you'll be wearing. We don't yet have a designated team swim suit, so bring what you have. Two suits and two towels. Also, make sure you bring some sort of sweatshirt to wear on the pool deck. Each of you should've received a list of other items to take. Remember, you can carry just one bag on the plane, so plan carefully. Pack lightly and tightly. Let your parents help you. They're the ones paying for you to take this trip, so please include them in your preparation. Yes, cell phones are all right, but no lap tops." He turned to Keith, his assistant. "What else?"

Sandy suddenly felt a pang of anxiety as he looked around at the young faces that, in turn, gazed back at him. Being responsible for these kids on a four-day, out-of-state trip entailed more than a few games. What if one of the youngsters got lost? Injured? Or worse? He'd had to schedule ground transportation and the flights for a group of a dozen. He'd made financial arrangements with each participating family, checked on insurance coverage, and more. Working with the polo people in the Philadelphia area, he'd had to make sure they'd received the entry fee for his team and a list of players. He'd bought tickets in advance for a bus tour of the big city. He'd finalized plans for his team members to stay in the homes of the host players, which proved to be a major chore. There seemed to be no end to what he was doing.

At the same time, he was putting in his usual 40-hour week as Head Lifeguard at the Downtown YMCA and coaching the water polo youngsters on a voluntary basis. Well, he told himself, I asked for it. Turning again to the 11- and 12-year-olds in front of him, Sandy said, "This is our final Saturday session in the college pool before we head to Philly next Friday morning. While we have our usual Tuesday and Thursday afternoon practices coming up this week at the Y, this is our last chance to scrimmage seven-per-side in a large, deep pool. So that's what we'll be doing today. Take your usual quarter-mile warm-up swim, and then I'll be passing out the caps so we can scrimmage for 45 minutes. It'll be tiring. Two things before we begin. First, you'll note that Hector is with us today. With him helping out, and with Beatrice having rejoined the team, we have enough to play seven-per-side even though Lexie won't be playing. I know she's here" – he tilted his head toward the young lady standing to his left – "and she's had her wrist cast removed, but I don't want her scrimmaging. She can swim some laps and take shooting practice with us at the Y on Tuesday and Thursday, and hopefully she'll be at her best, fully recovered, when we fly to Philly. For the rest of you, I want you to go at it hard today. Do you hear me? I said HARD! Yes, even when you're becoming exhausted. As the refs, Keith and I may not call some of the fouls we see because I want you to be ready for rough play next weekend. So play hard. Be tough. Now let's go."

As the scrimmage progressed, Sandy saw that the play was sloppy. The kids simply weren't used to playing seven-per-side. They'd done it a few times but not enough to become proficient. The passing was all right. The guarding was good. But the timing was off, and few shots were taken. Goalies Nona and Jose could have stayed in bed for all the action they were seeing. As the scrimmage approached an end, Sandy pulled his usual stunt. He put all the girls on one side, all the boys on the other. The two groups, separated by gender, seemed to perform better that way. Once previously, when the girls had scored a goal or two against the boys in a scrimmage, Ellery had chastised his teammates. "Don't let them do that," he shouted in frustration. They're mere girls." To which Warner had replied, "Well, girls aren't so mere any more." The two teams finally were doing a bit better, and after spending the last 15 minutes reviewing the extra-man situation, both offensively and defensively, neither of which the players did well, Sandy blew his whistle. "That's it for today, lads and lassies. Y'all did great," he fibbed. "Get showered and dressed. I'll be waiting outside in case your parents have any questions for me."

As the kids ambled away, Sandy whispered to Keith, "Let's hope we play a lot better next weekend or we'll be blown out of the Wilson High School pool."

* * * * *

When it came to selecting the 10 youngsters to go on the trip, there was good news and bad news, Sandy rationalized. The good news was that Lexie appeared to have recovered from her wrist injury and would be one of the six girls going, the others being Nona, Delia, Savannah, Princess, and Wanda. He was leaving two 11-year-olds, Beatrice and Janis, at home, along with Cindy, the newcomer from the Y's swim classes. "Your turn will come," he told them.

As for the boys, the bad news was that Junior, who played the hole set position, was ill. His parents had called Sandy and said, "He could go, but he has a fever, and we don't want to take a chance on him becoming sicker when he's out of town. Sorry." Thus the four boys heading to Philadelphia were Jose, Ben, Ellery, and Warner.

Eight of the players, Sandy believed, would hold their own against whatever opponents they faced. The weak links, so to speak, were the brother and sister duo of Warner and Wanda. But they'd practiced hard since the program started and deserved the trip. Furthermore, their affluent parents were not only paying the way for the two youngsters of their own but also had given Sandy an extra check in the amount of $300. "It's anonymous," they said, "but you can use it for any of your players who might need some financial assistance." One of the girls did, so Sandy was grateful. "I'm sure," Kristina informed him, "that they'll use it as a tax write-off, but that's the way the system works."

Now, sitting in the local airport on Friday morning, Sandy looked around at the group that was heading north. They'd all arisen early from their various homes and driven to the airport, arriving shortly after 6:00 a.m. in order to check-in for the 7:00

a.m. flight to Charlotte, where they'd transfer to another plane that would take them to Philly. For most, this would be their initial venture via airplane so, as expected, there was a lot of excited chattering. The parents were still there, waiting apprehensively for the departure. Sandy turned to Kristina, who was going along as the chaperone. "This was my dream several months ago. When I told the parents about traveling to Philly, I never thought it'd actually happen."

"Nor did I," she replied. "Yet here we are. Let's hope that everything turns out for the best over the weekend."

Sandy had debated as to whom he should select as his assistant for this adventure. At first, he'd decided to take Keith, who'd been helping him at the youth practices. Then he realized he needed a woman to serve as chaperone for the young girls. He'd asked the mothers of his team members if one of them wanted to go. Two replied in the affirmative, but their own youngsters, who were making the trip, argued against it. "This is for US," the kids heatedly told the moms. "Stay home. Let us do it on our own." Typical 12-year-olds. The two mothers backed off, leaving Sandy with a choice between Sabrina, his sister, and Kristina, his girlfriend. He favored Sabrina so as to avoid any appearance of impropriety, but his father said, "Sabrina's only 17. She's too young herself to be a chaperone, and she's legally too young to rent a car, which you'll be doing. I suggest you take Kristina. She's just turned 21, and she has her head on straight. I think her parents will let her make the trip, even if it takes some of the money she's saved for college. Just make sure the two of you bed down in separate rooms!"

"Yes, here we are," Sandy smiled at Kristina in the airport as it was announced that the flight to Charlotte was boarding. "And here we go."

With the weather cooperating – bright and sunny with nothing stormy in the forecast – the flights to Charlotte and then to Philadelphia were uneventful. Sandy and Kristina tried to remain calm as the 10 youngsters were fidgety and nervous and unable to sit still. "Take it easy," the coach cautioned Lexie. "Protect your wrist. We don't need another accident."

It was approaching noon when the second flight started descending into the Philadelphia airport. "We're exactly on time," the captain announced over the intercom. "The weather here is great. Hope you enjoy your visit to the City of Brotherly Love."

"Yeah, yeah. I don't expect the opposing teams will show us much love," Sandy remarked to Kristina, "but maybe, hopefully, our kids will hold their own." He'd hoped that some of the parents of the host team, in whose homes they'd be staying, would arrange to meet them at the airport. But Tom, the coach at Wilson High School, had told him previously, "You're arriving on a Friday, which is a work day for our parents and a school day for our children. You'll have to rent a couple of cars and come to West Lawn on your own. I suggest you stop for lunch along the way. Your kids will be hungry. We're not far from the airport, but with all you have to do – deplaning, picking up the rental vehicles, stopping to eat – it'll take you two hours to get here. When you do, we'll take over."

Driving one rental car occupied by Wanda and the four boys while Kristina drove the second vehicle containing the five other girls, Sandy & Co. reached Wilson High School at 2:30 p.m. They were greeted by Tom, the WHS coach, and Rudy, the Superintendent of District Schools, who was also the leader of prep water polo in the State of Pennsylvania. "Let's go see the pool where you'll be playing," the visitors were told, "and by that time, the families that'll be serving as your hosts should be here."

The indoor pool proved to be spacious and, as one of the Western North Carolina girls uttered, "Spectacular!" It was larger than the two-pool Aquatic Center at the Downtown YMCA, not even counting the seating arrangement for 500 spectators. "We've just re-opened the pool after having suffered through a one-year renovation project," said Tom. "We had to go to other pools in the area to practice all that time. It's nice to be back in business here."

"Sort of like what we do," Kristina interjected, "because none of our public high schools back home has a pool. We use the Y pools and various community pools and a local college pool, wherever we can squeeze in a few hours of practice time. It's logistically difficult and has been that way ever since I can remember."

"Well," Sandy said to the youngsters who stood beside him on the deck, "don't be alarmed. It's still chlorinated water that's in this pool, same as back home, and we're still playing the same game, water polo." Taking a vial from his pocket, he poured its contents into the high school pool. "This is water from our Y pools. You can see how it mixes with the water here. Y'all can do the same tomorrow when you return to play. Jump in, feel how your body melds with the water, as always, and how good it feels, and remember how much you love playing water polo, whether it's at home or here or elsewhere. It's your game. Do your best."

Sandy spent the night in the home of the Superintendent of Schools, Rudy, and his wife, Sue. In addition to being top educators, they were water polo enthusiasts. Rudy had started playing recreationally as a teenager and continued to play at West Chester University. Taking up coaching, he'd led the local boys to 10 state and Eastern championships, with his teams once posting a winning streak of more than 100 consecutive victories. Sue had helped promote women's and girls' water polo. Their two children, now grown, had been high school All-Americans who then starred in collegiate competition. Although he was now serving as a school administrator, Rudy remained involved with the sport. When the local teams, playing under the aegis of Kingfish Water Polo, recently traveled to the West Coast to compete against the best California clubs, Rudy and Sue went along. No wonder Sandy, Rudy, and Sue stayed awake until midnight, talking about water polo in every aspect of the game. It was tough arising earlier than usual for the second day in a row, but with his team scheduled to play at 9:00 a.m. on Saturday, Sandy knew it was time to tackle the task at hand.

Walking into Wilson High School as his kids also arrived from the various homes in which they were staying, the Y coach felt his heart starting to pound. Was his team up to the challenge? It would be sink or swim. Hopefully, the latter.

* * * *

"We've not even started to play, but already our kids are dead tired," Kristina observed. She had spent the preceding night at the home of Tom, the WHS coach, and his family. "He's a good guy," Kristina told Sandy on Saturday morning as they watched their kids swimming a few laps to warm-up. "He's the one who talked American Water Polo into letting us enter this tourney. He was a collegiate All-American in both swimming and water polo and is already in several Halls of Fame."

"Let's hope our players can show him they know the difference between a water polo ball and a hockey puck. They look like they're still sleeping right now which shouldn't be surprising after they lost so many hours of sleep the last two nights, plus doing all the traveling. I guess I should've realized this would happen to young 12-year-olds."

Moments later, it was time for the game to begin. The YMCA entry was playing in the 12-and-under category for beginning-level coed teams, and Sandy decided to start Jose in the goal, Ben back on defense with Delia also helping out defensively, Ellery and Princess and Savannah in mid-pool, and Lexie up front in the hole set position. The teams lined up at opposite ends of the pool. The referee blew his whistle and tossed out the ball. Delia sprinted and captured the ball and passed back to Princess. She threw an errant pass that was intercepted. The opposing team raced down the pool and took a weak shot at the goal which Jose easily handled. His pass was then intercepted. The opposing team made one or two passes and shot again, missed again. "They're fairly fast," Sandy said, "but I don't think they can handle the ball any better than our kids."

It was back and forth throughout the first quarter. Sandy's squad continued its sloppy play on offense but was able to turn away every attack by the opposing team. At the break, Sandy gathered his group around him and said, "Get the ball to Lexie. I think she can score. If she's not open, I want you, Princess, to shoot. The other team is mostly boys, and they're guarding our boys. Their two girls can't match up with our girls. Okay, now, you're doing great on defense, and I want you, Jose and Ben and Ellery, to keep on guarding closely. When we get the ball, Delia, you pass it to Lexie or Princess. You're all warmed-up now. Let's play water polo."

Once again Delia swam swiftly to grab the ball in mid-pool at the beginning of the second stanza. She passed to Princess, who passed accurately back to her. Sensing her opponent was a young and not-very-good substitute, Delia immediately dribbled down the pool, stopped at the four-yard line, reared back, and fired at the cage. Score! "So much for following my instructions," Sandy said with a smirk.

The Northern team took several more shots and hit on one, evening the score. Then Princess used her strong arm to send a rocket into the opposing cage that put the Western North Carolina contingent in the lead. With time running out, the team finally managed to get the ball to Lexie, who all this time had been loosely guarded. She turned and lofted a shot into the far corner of the cage. "Looks like her wrist is okay," Kristina stated softly.

The third quarter was almost a repeat of the second. This time it was Savannah who led off with the scoring. The opposing team again took several shots and made one. Then the YMCA team passed the ball into Lexie, and once more she turned, elbowed her way clear, and aimed at one corner of the cage. As the goalie moved in that direction, Lexie promptly powered a shot into the other corner.

"Warner and Wanda," Sandy shouted, "hop in and replace Ellery and Savannah. Play tough on defense. Don't let your opponent score. That's an order." The brother and sister duo did as instructed, and the period ended with Sandy's squad leading, 5-to-2.

Looking at Kristina and shaking his head, Sandy said, "I'm putting Nona in the goal for the fourth quarter. "I don't like having boys shooting at a girl goalie, but we'll just have to see how she does."

"I think both teams are running out of steam," Kristina declared. "They're still faster, but we pass the ball better. I think we're better on defense, too. Let's hope our kids can hold on."

Sure enough, seeing a girl playing goalie, the opposing team shot several times from the outside, and once of them trickled off Nona's hands into the cage. "Ellery and Savannah," Sandy said, "go back in for the twins. Get the ball to Lexie." It took several exchanges of the ball with neither team scoring before the ball reached Lexie. She turned and prepared to shoot when two opposing players jumped her. In an instant, she passed to unguarded Delia, who pumped in the clinching shot. "There's less than a minute to go," Sandy shouted to his players. "Play defense. Toughen up."

Ben refused to let an opposing player get off a shot and was sent into the penalty area for 30 seconds by the referee for his over-aggressive efforts. The other team now had a one-player advantage. "Hands up!" Sandy shouted. "You know what to do." The opposing team wasn't quite sure what to do but somehow managed to get off a shot that hit home as the whistle sounded, ending the game. But it didn't matter. Sandy looked at the scoreboard just to make sure he had it right. Yes, there it was. His team had won, 6-to-4.

"Okay, gang, that was great. Now line up and slap hands with the other team. That's how the game ends, with a show of good sportsmanship. C'mon now." After sending the Y youngsters to the locker rooms – "take a long, warm shower and get dressed, and then we'll go get an early lunch somewhere" – Sandy and Kristina were relaxing when approached by Tom, the host coach. "Your kids played well," he said. "I can see they're not competitive swimmers, but they know the game for being only 12 years old."

"Yeah," Sandy acknowledged. "We seem to be doing it backwards. Our YMCA has a strong youth swim squad that's developed a number of national champions in recent years, and in order to resuscitate the Y's water polo program, we agreed not to interfere with the competitive swimmers. I recruited out of the swim classes. We spent the autumn and winter months practicing just twice weekly in the Y's small, shallow pool. This spring we've added a third practice in the local college pool which is larger, deeper. Since the beginning, I've been teaching the basics of water polo, and we're just starting to work on swimming speed and stamina. But we're making progress."

"They're a good group of kids," Kristina added.

"My parents all said your youngsters were well-behaved at their houses last night," Tom stated, "and when called this morning, they all got up and dressed promptly. But I have to warn you. This afternoon you'll be facing a tougher opponent. You'll need to have your team ready to play."

That night, when Sandy returned to the home of Rudy and Sue, she asked, "How did your team do today?"

"We squeezed out a win this morning, 6-to-4. But in our afternoon game, we stunk, frankly. The other team was bigger, and our kids were tired. We couldn't keep up. We have a good girl playing hole set, and she scored three times, but we ended up losing, 7-to-5. It wasn't pretty."

"Who'd you play?" Rudy wanted to know. When Sandy told him, Rudy replied, "That was one of the strongest 12-and-under teams in this area. Maybe you'll do better tomorrow."

"I hope so."

But it wasn't to be. The YMCA team from Western North Carolina faced another worthy opponent on Sunday morning. Watching the game, Sandy turned to Kristina and said, rather dejectedly, "Our kids are playing fairly well, probably better than yesterday. I can't believe how good the opposing team is. For 11- and 12-year-olds, they can *really* play water polo. Looks to me like they belong in the division for experienced teams."

"Well, you brought our kids here to learn, to improve," Kristina said, "and this is an excellent opportunity for them to do so."

When the game was over, Sandy didn't have to look at the scoreboard to know the result. It was 10-to-5, and his team was NOT on top. Lexie had again scored three goals from her hole set spot. "We're sure lucky her wrist healed and she was able to make the trip," Kristina pointed out, "or we've have been totally embarrassed."

Gathering his group together for lunch at a nearby restaurant, Sandy gave his weary and withdrawn players a pep talk. They sat quietly and picked at their food as they listened. "I know you're disappointed, but you shouldn't be. You're trying hard, and you're playing better with each game, and that's all I can ask. With our two defeats, we're out of the championship bracket, but we still have one game to go this afternoon, and if we win, you'll take home the consolation crown. That would be a terrific achievement. So perk up, eat up, and when we get back to the pool, lie down and rest until it's time for our game. Then let's play hard, play together, and WIN."

After the team they faced in the morning contest provided them with such stiff opposition, the afternoon opponent proved to be much less skilled. They too were tired and discouraged from their losses, and they weren't very good at playing polo. Contrariwise, the Sandy Ballers of the past demonstrated they'd learned to play water polo somewhat effectively, at least against this opponent.

Goalies Jose and Nona both performed well, aided by the defensive efforts of Ben, who was rough, tough, and Delia, who was quick, smart. The mid-pool players, Ellery, Princess, Savannah, Warner, and Wanda, seemed to be swimming better than ever. Maybe the other team is just out of it, Sandy thought to himself. Up front, Lexie was being double-teamed – at least that's what the opposition was trying to do – but it didn't matter. She still scored a couple and passed to her teammates who were scoring, as well. It was 3-to-0, 5-to-2, and then 7-to-3 entering the fourth quarter. "Okay, now," Sandy stated. "Let's have Jose back in as goalie, and in the field I want Ben, Delia, Savannah, Wanda, Princess, and Lexie. We have the final five minutes to play, and while I know you're dead tired, you need to crank it up one more time. Good guarding, good passing, strong shooting. Let's take home the consolation title."

It wasn't all that Sandy had hoped, but it wasn't too bad. The guarding was fair, the passing fair, and the shooting fair. When he moaned a time or two, Kristina reminded him that it was his team's fourth official game in two days. "They've given it everything they have. Give 'em credit."

Midway through the period, Delia passed into Lexie who swirled and shot and scored. The opposing team retaliated with a score, and Sandy shouted, "Toughen up. The game's not over yet." His team again passed the ball into Lexie, who was hammered. The opposing player was ejected for 30 seconds. With an extra player, the visitors from Western North Carolina showed that they'd listened somewhat to their coach's instructions back home. They managed to set up with three in the front row and three in back, and with little opposition thrown at them at this stage of the game, it was easy for Princess to use her strong right arm to score from six yards out.

When the whistle blew signifying the game's conclusion, Sandy couldn't help but look at the scoreboard. There it was. His Sandy Ballers had 9, the opposing team 4. All in all, they'd won two, lost two. Not too bad. There were still two games to be contested in the championship bracket for the more experienced youngsters. Sandy and his crew, after they'd showered and dressed, watched somewhat impatiently but cheered when the home team, Kingfish Water Polo, coached by Tom, finished first.

Eventually the awards were passed out, with trophies presented to the top teams and medals going to the 14 players – seven boys, seven girls – named to the all-tournament lineup. Sandy was pleased to see that the sanctioning organization, American Water Polo, was recognizing the girls separately for their having competed in a coed tourney against the boys. One of the girls selected was Lexie. She was among the scoring leaders with 11 goals in her four games. "She's a whiz, no doubt about it," Sandy said. "I think Delia should've been chosen, too," Kristina commented. "Maybe next time."

It was quiet on Sunday night in the various homes in which Sandy, Kristina, and the kids were staying. Everyone was exhausted, the hosts and the visitors alike. Besides, Monday would be another work day, school day, for the West Lawn residents. The plan was for the families to bring the kids to school at the usual time on Monday morning. There, the Western North Carolina contingent would reunite, hop into the two vehicles they were renting, and drive back to Philadelphia. "There'll be a lot of traffic heading into Philly this morning," Superintendent Rudy warned them. "Be careful. Take your time."

"We enjoyed having you," Coach Tom exclaimed. "Hope you can come again."

"I can't begin to tell you how much we appreciate your hospitality," Sandy said emphatically. "You've made it a wonderful experience for our kids. Thank you, thank you."

The return to Philadelphia was, as Rudy had anticipated, fraught with speedy and careless drivers on the overcrowded highway, and both Sandy and Kristina were relieved when they reached their destination, which was a bus depot. "We complain that our roads back home are becoming jammed with drivers," Kristina stated, "but it's nothing like this."

"I'm glad we can sit and relax on the bus tour," Sandy said, "but we still have to drive to the airport this afternoon." He'd arranged in advance for the group of 12 to take a two-hour tour of Philadelphia's most important historical sites. They'd be riding in a large double-decker open air bus. Luckily the weather remained dry and clear, and with a blue sky above, Sandy and Kristina smiled at each other as they watched the exuberance of the youngsters as the bus took them from one landmark to another.

After an hour of sight-seeing, Warner and Wanda stood up and announced, "We're hungry."

Several others chimed in with Savannah saying, "Yeah, we were rushed this morning, and all I had was a small bowl of cereal."

"Not to worry," Sandy said. "We'll be getting off in a few minutes when we reach the Liberty Bell, and I'll have a big surprise." Sure enough, after the group climbed down from the top deck of the bus and spent 10 minutes looking closely at the famous Liberty Bell, Sandy stated, "Let's take a walk." Three blocks later, they arrived at a restaurant which had a short line in front. "We can't leave Philadelphia without tasting the world-renowned Philly cheesesteak sandwiches, and this place, Campo's Deli, is supposed to have the best. They also have hoagies and other things. So let's chow down. But don't take too long. We have to catch the next tour bus that'll be coming along in 30 minutes."

Excitedly, the kids joined the line and, one after another, placed their orders. One of the girls whispered to Kristina, "I don't have any more money." Overhearing, Sandy said, "You played so well on both Saturday and Sunday that it's my privilege to pick up your check. Just give it to me."

The day continued to unfold. The dozen travelers ate, with each expressing an opinion about how good the cheesesteaks were, or not, and boarded the next bus, completing the two-hour tour of the city. They packed themselves into the two rental cars which, with their luggage included, had them sitting on top of each other. "Hang on," the coach said. "We don't have far to go, just to the airport."

It wasn't as simple as it sounded. The bumper-to-bumper traffic. The unloading. Turning in the rental vehicles. The check-in, which was a hassle. Finally they seemed to have everything accomplished. Sandy called the kids together and said, "We have one more thing to do before our flight leaves in an hour. Form a circle and hold hands. Now bow your heads." He spoke softly, thanking a Higher Power for keeping them safe. He then offered thanks for the parents from back home and from the hosting club. He expressed his appreciation for the tournament promoters and officials for their efforts, for the YMCA and its support over the past nine months, and for the young team members themselves not only for their water polo performance but also their good behavior over the weekend. He closed by saying, "You're a great group. I love each one of you."

After the youngsters collapsed into various airport chairs and seats and became immersed in their hand-held computer games, Kristina said, "That was nice, Sandy. Very nice."

"Well, it's the Y's way, isn't it? And by the way, thanks to YOU for coming on this trip. And for coming into my life."

CHAPTER NINE

SUMMER SUCCESSES

The letter was awaiting him when he returned home. It was totally unexpected. It was an invitation from the coach of the U.S. national and Olympic men's water polo team to attend a training camp in California in July. The coach wrote, "We're looking to expand our program to include promising players from around the country. You, Sandy, impressed our staff when you were here. With your size, strength, swimming speed, and water polo skills, you are just the type of prospect we're seeking. The training camp will be held for four weeks at our new site, which is located at the Santa Ana YMCA swimming pool complex in southern California. You are responsible for providing your travel costs, but once you've arrived, we will cover your housing and meals for the entirety of the camp. You will need money for your incidental expenses. If interested in attending, please let me know within 72 hours of receiving this invitation. My staff and I hope to be seeing you soon."

WOW. What an opportunity, Sandy thought. But I'll have to get back in shape. Quickly. I can do it. I'll be completing the full year I promised to give to the YMCA here, and I'll have time to train someone else to serve as the Head Lifeguard. Two or three of the guards are experienced enough to take my place. As for the young water poloists, my assistant, Keith, can step in. He knows what to do. Yes, yes, it's all falling into place.

"What'll you tell Kristina?" his sister asked.

"She'll understand. It's just for a month. Then ..."

"Then what? If you make the U.S. training team, you'll be staying in California. If you don't make it, you'll be starting all over again, either here or there. You'd better think it over very, very carefully, Sandy."

He wanted to go. He slept on it for two nights. He had a discussion with his parents, who echoed Sabrina's concerns. "Your sister may be younger than you, but she's a smart young lady," his dad said. "You'd be wise to listen to her advice."

"Have you discussed the situation with Kristina?" his mother wondered.

"No."

"And the people at the YMCA?"

"No."

"And your water polo kids and their parents?"

"Not yet."

"This isn't just about you, Sandy. A lot of people are going to be affected if you decide to go."

"But it's such a great opportunity," he insisted. "Once in a lifetime and all that."

When he finally told Kristina about the invitation, she agreed with him. "You have to go, Sandy. I don't want to be the one standing in your way." Yet he could hear how her voice cracked. He could see the wrinkles of dismay on her forehead and how her mouth turned down at the corners.

It was certainly a tough decision. As the 72-hour deadline approached, he still hadn't told Tina and Lydia at the YMCA, even when he saw them as he continued serving as Head Lifeguard. He'd given the water poloists a week off after returning home from the trip to Philadelphia, but he'd have to face them sooner or later. Sitting by himself on the familiar bench at the riverside park where he and Kristina had enjoyed such togetherness in the recent past, Sandy knew the time had arrived for him to decide. This is something I need to do, he told himself, something I hoped for when I went to college in California, when I stayed there for an additional two years to practice with the best at Los Alamitos, an opportunity to become one of the best myself. They want me. How can I turn it down? He reached for his cell phone and called the coach of the U.S. national and Olympic team.

* * * * *

"Only time will tell," said Champ, the former YMCA Director of Aquatics and swimming and water polo coach, with whom Sandy was again having a lunch meeting. Handling his usual order, a club sandwich, with deftness, the ol' coach continued. "When I was exactly your age, 25, I too had to make a major decision. I'd been drafted into the Army when I was 20, spent a year with the UN occupation forces in Korea as the war there was winding down, returned to the U.S. and was married, attended college back home in the Midwest for a couple of years, and received several job offers. I'd done some writing about swimming, and a new magazine, *Swimming World*, located in southern California, offered me a position as assistant editor. Believe me, I was tempted. But instead I accepted a beginning-level job with the YMCA. I'd been a Y member since my teen days, even competing in the Swimming Nationals when I was 18, and I appreciated the organization's expertise in aquatics – recognized as the best in the world at that time – and emphasis on the principles of Christianity. You know the rest of the story."

He paused, looked off into space for a full minute, and then resumed his recollections of the past. "I had a 40-year YMCA career that took me from Minnesota to Iowa to Illinois and finally here, to the mountains of Western North Carolina. I had several excellent opportunities to become an exec, which I never accepted. Didn't want to sit behind a desk, even when I was in my 50s and 60s. Liked being in the pool, amidst the action. Still do in my old age."

"So you think I made the right choice?" Sandy demanded.

"As I said, only time will tell, but here you are, in somewhat of a beginning-level aquatics job at the Downtown YMCA. You're not married, but you seem to be involved in a meaningful relationship. You've just turned down an opportunity to go back to California because, for whatever your reasons might be, you want to remain at home. You're involved with water polo, a sport you love, and you have one advantage that I didn't have. I wasn't introduced to the game until I was 25 and beginning my full-time Y career, while you've been playing locally and even nationally for a number of years. On the other hand, I had one advantage that you don't have. When I was starting out, the Y's top leaders – Arnold,

Atkinson, Cox, Cureton, deBarbadillo, Empleton, Friermood, Gilchrist, Griffin, Golay, Havlick, Hummer, Miller, Rosewarren, Stanwood, Steinhaus, Tanner, Thomason, Thraillkill, Welch, Wortman, and many others you probably never heard of – were enthused about developing a lot of exciting new character-building athletic activities. This included water polo and scuba diving, to mention two that attracted my attention. Nowadays, let's face it, the Y's aquatics programming isn't what it used to be, with the sole exception of competitive swimming. The organization is currently more focused on health and wellness, on fitness for adults and childcare for families, which is what most communities need. It's okay. The YMCA changes with the times, which is why it's been the world's most successful social service agency for over 150 years. So I'll tell you this, Sandy. If you intend to have a career with the Y, you can pursue your own specialty, whether it's water polo or something else, but you'd better be willing and able to branch out and do a dozen other things, as well."

"That's really great advice, Champ."

"Well, once again I'm sorry for having lectured so long. Tell me about your trip to Philadelphia. I have good memories of taking a team there, staying in the homes of the host families, like you did, and playing in a tourney in a big high school pool. But we had separate divisions for boys and girls, nothing coed."

Sandy spent the next 20 minutes bringing the ol' coach up to date on all that'd taken place on the four-day adventure to play at Wilson High School in West Lawn, a Philly suburb. In conclusion, he said, "I'm amazed at how well these younger kids, just 11 and 12, can play polo. In swimming nowadays, the times that the 12-year-olds are recording are absolutely fantastic. When I watch various sports on TV or on the internet, such as gymnastics or basketball or soccer or Little League baseball and softball, the best of the young ones seem to perform with a high degree of skill. Certainly with more competence than I had when I was that age."

"It's a different world, that's for sure. Kids are maturing earlier, and there are more opportunities for them to learn to play sports. When I was growing up, it was all sandlot. We organized ourselves without any adult involvement. That actually wasn't such a bad thing as it taught us self-sufficiency. But now there are facilities we never dreamed of and well-paid youth coaches and competition galore. It's trickled down from the major sports to water polo. Which is why USA Water Polo has a Splash Ball program for 10-and-unders and you're teaching 11- and 12-year-olds at the Y."

"Yeah," Sandy agreed. "I love all my kids. They've really grown up since we started last September. I mean that literally. Most are an inch or two taller and 10 pounds heavier. Stronger. The difference between ages 11 and 12, especially amongst the girls I have, is impressive. They still have a ways to go to become good water poloists, but right now they're on the right track."

"Sounds like you're happy you decided to stay here, Sandy. What's your summer season look like? That was always the most enjoyable time of the year for our water poloists in the 1960s, 1970s, 1980s."

Sandy sat back in his seat and scanned the restaurant, which was a busy place. He took a sip of iced tea and munched down the last bite of his salmon. "Unfortunately, Champ, we don't have all the nearby competition nowadays that you had in the past. Water polo continues to grow in most places, although not here in the Carolinas, at least on the youth level. But I've discovered there are kids learning the game in Raleigh. Someone sent me a newspaper article the other day about Raleigh having had three or four teams playing polo for the past several summers. Not sure of the ages, but the article mentioned that children as young as 10, 11, and 12 were participating. They have two Saturday clinics scheduled for July and hope to conduct a small youth tournament in August. This may be one opportunity for us. Also, I plan to run a clinic of my own with the help of our local Masters club."

"How's it look for practice time? That was always a problem for us in the past."

"Good news. First, we have about 12 new kids pre-registered for our summer program. I don't know how many can swim, but we'll find out. Second, the YMCA Piranhas swim squad always moves outside to a couple of 50-meter community pools for their summer practicing, which opens up more time for us at the Downtown YMCA. We'll still be there on Tuesdays and Thursdays but for two hours, from 6:00 to 8:00 p.m., instead of just the one hour we've had in the past. We'll also continue to have the college pool on Saturday mornings for 90 minutes. I'd like to get the kids outside for another practice each week, maybe in the nice pool at the YMCA's Blue Ridge Assembly, but I don't want to push the families too much. Three practices per week for 11- and 12-year-olds should be enough, don't you think?"

Champ laughed. "Well, Sandy, you know the Californians, probably better than I do. They'll have their young kids practicing two hours every day of the week in some of the fanciest pools on the planet. As always, it's tough to keep up with them. But strictly from an educational standpoint, I agree with you that for 11- and 12-year-olds, three practices weekly, if conducted correctly, should be sufficient. Everyone needs time to enjoy other activities in life, yourself included. Say, whose turn is it to pick up today's check?"

* * * * *

Ages. Birth dates. Family vacations. I'm in over my head, Sandy decided. Here we are, entering the busy summer season in our Downtown YMCA pools, with more lifeguarding chores to be performed than usual, and I'm worried about the kids' water polo program. First things first, he reminded himself. I'm being paid to serve as Head Lifeguard, and nothing is more important than maintaining safety in the Aquatic Center. He called a meeting of his guards on a Saturday afternoon, a time that set several of them to grumbling. "I'm sorry," he explained to the group gathered around him on the outside deck of the Aquatic Center, "but we have to get this done."

Looking around at the circle of faces, he continued, "As most of you know, the summer schedule is different from what we're used to. I started here last July, and I jumped into the middle of it. There are definitely more children coming to swim in the summertime than during the school year, both for the various lessons and the family sessions. It's always been that way. I was looking through some old records recently and learned that on a July day in 1985, when the YMCA had just the one lap pool, there were 364 swimmers in attendance. About two-thirds were kids, mainly day campers. That was a pool record at the time. This and a few other days of similar overcrowding convinced the Y leaders that another pool was needed. So the second warm-water therapy-type pool was added in 1986.

"But that's all behind us now. We have a great group of 12 experienced lifeguards" – he took time to look into every face – "and I'm proud of you. Each one of you. We have three or four additional guards who'll be working with you over the summer months. You've already met them. I'm doing some separate training with them. Please welcome them and show them the ropes." Sandy paused, caught his breath, and carried on. "Here's something I haven't told you yet. We had a small group of seven enrolled in our spring junior lifesaving course. I've assigned each one to a week of on-the-job training during June and July. So they'll be here, a different one each week, to learn from you. They're young and impressionable, and it's your responsibility to set a good example..."

For another hour, Sandy and his guards shared information and ideas about how to make the forthcoming summer season "the best ever," as stated by Meredith, one of the guards. At the end, Sandy said, "Oh, one more thing. As if I've not thrown enough at you, don't forget that in August we'll be having the next Lifeguard Games, in which you'll be competing against the guards from the other Y branches. So stay in shape, and stay sharp."

Afterwards, he and Kristina visited a downtown ice cream parlor, and as they sat on the stools and enjoyed each other's company, as well as the flavor of their choice, Sandy asked, "I wasn't too demanding of the guards, was I?"

"Not at all. You're the boss, and you should set the tone. As you've said many times before, safety is our main concern in aquatics, and we all need to be reminded of that from time to time, especially with the busy summer classes and family swims facing us. And after all, that's your job, serving as Head Lifeguard. It's the reason you decided to pass up the national training camp in California, isn't it?"

Detecting a touch of irony in her voice, Sandy chuckled. "No, not exactly."

"So what was the reason?"

"I'm looking at it, er, her." Before Kristina could comment, Sandy added, "Also, I feel obligated to continue working with the Y kids. They and their parents seem to have bought in to what I'm trying to do, and I just can't turn my back on them for my own selfish purposes. But I have to admit that coaching is tougher than I realized."

"How so?"

"It's not the practices or the games. It's the little things that must be done, the little annoyances that crop up. For example, if we're planning to keep on fielding a 12-and-under team, or teams, I need to know each player's exact age and birth date. I've just realized that Ben will be aging up in August and Savannah in September. They'll be turning 13. Where will they fit in? Do I keep them in the program, or not? Do I have someone ready to take their places in the 12-and-unders? I'm also trying to get the details on the summer youth water polo program over in Raleigh. On whether or not they'll be hosting a youth tourney in August as they've done the last two or three summers. I need to know what they have planned because it's imperative that I inform our parents. I don't want them taking their summer vacations at the same time. There's more, but you get what I'm saying."

The two sat in silence for awhile as the crowd swirled around them and music played in the background. Eventually Kristina spoke up, "Did you take a beating moneywise from the trip to Philadelphia?"

Sandy shrugged. "I put about $5,000 on my credit card. That's counting the air fare for 12 of us, the rental of two cars, the bus tour, some meals, and a few incidentals. Luckily the Y's board of directors picked up the entry fee, which was helpful. We also received the nice $300 donation from one of the families. I've been repaid the cost of the $350 plane tickets by six of the participating families, plus you, Kristina. Three other families are repaying me month by month. I doubt that I'll be getting anything from the final family, but I'm using the donation to cover that. I paid my own way, of course, and will probably bite the bullet when it comes to the car rentals and bus tour. But that's okay. I'm not complaining."

"You're a good guy, Sandy," stated Kristina, giving his arm a tight hug.

"And I have a good girlfriend," he replied, returning the hug with even more conviction.

* * * * *

With 12 new players having signed up for the summer, more than he anticipated, and 16 continuing to participate – Lexie, Delia, Savannah, Princess, Nona, Wanda, Janis, Beatrice, Cindy for the girls and Ben, Jose, Junior, Ellery, Warner, Clayton, Leland for the boys – he had more than he could handle in a single group. On Tuesday and Thursday evenings, he used the 6:00 to 7:00 time in the lap pool for the newcomers. He had the more advanced group coming at the same time, and while he was teaching the newbies in the pool, he had his assistant, Keith, showing videos of various 12-and-under games from the past two Junior Olympics in California to the 16 so-called veterans. While the schedule indicated that the more advanced group was to practice from 7:00 to 8:00, Sandy usually chased the dozen new participants out of the pool 15 minutes early and started the Sandy Ballers of the past a bit early, as soon as their video viewing was done. They've earned it, he explained. He also limited the Saturday morning sessions at the college pool to those who'd been practicing there previously. I'm hoping to take them to a tourney in Raleigh, he said, and they need all the time they can get in a larger, deeper pool.

As it turned out, the trip in August to Raleigh actually materialized, which was somewhat of a shock. It was scheduled for the same weekend that Sandy was planning to conduct the Lifeguard Games, at which his crew from the Downtown YMCA would be taking on the guards from the Y's three other pools. "Wouldn't you know!" he exclaimed. "I can't ask the polo people in Raleigh to readjust their schedule. We've have to reschedule here." The lifeguards groaned, and Kristina smiled and said, "Just another one of those little things you mentioned, Sandy. The little annoyances that crop up. Deal with it."

It was proving difficult to keep all of his young players moving in the same direction, but thankfully, the successes of the YMCA's youth swim squad gave Sandy an opportunity to motivate his players. In late July, one of the Piranhas won two races at the Y's Long Course National Championships, and the girls' medley relay quartet, averaging just 15 years of age, which had reached the consolation finals at the Short Course Nationals in April, this time made it to the championship finals. Sandy's sister, who'd been part of the medley quartet for the Short Course competition, had been replaced by a younger and faster swimmer for the Long Course races at Indianapolis. Overall, the local team had finished a commendable 14th out of 150 teams entered in the competition and 600 Y teams scattered across the continent. "Look at what they've accomplished," Sandy pointed out to his young athletes. "In recent years, the Y swimmers have had four, maybe five, national winners, and as a team, they've placed as high as eighth nationally. If they can do it, so can you."

"I'll bet we can beat 'em in water polo," said Ellery.

"Well, maybe," Sandy conceded, "but right now let's worry about how we'll do in Raleigh."

The worrying was unnecessary. The teams from Raleigh weren't nearly as good as those they'd faced at Wilson High School in May. They were comprised mostly of recreational swimmers who played a little water polo during the summer months. The older Raleigh youngsters, ages 13 to 17, had acquired some skills over the past several years, but most of the younger ones, ages 9 to 12, were just learning.

The one-day event was held in the newly-refurbished and spacious Sonner Pool. As he'd done on the trip to the Philly area, Sandy brought along a vial of water from the YMCA pools back home, which he emptied into the pool in Raleigh. "This makes it ours," he declared. His team of boys, to which he'd added 14-year-old Hector and then supplemented with three newcomers in order to fill out the roster, won its two games by scores of 10-to-6 and 8-to-4. Junior, who'd missed the trip to Philly in May due to an illness, was the leading scorer.

The girls from the mountains had an even easier time of it, taking their two games by decisive margins of 17-to-6 and 14-to-4. It could have been worse, but Sandy substituted freely. In the third quarter of the second game, Sandy's assistant, Keith Cartwright, said, "The girls are looking good." As he spoke, Nona blocked one of the few shots allowed by the mountain team's defense and passed to Wanda who, in turn, passed to Delia, who dribbled the ball down the pool. She passed cross-pool to Savannah who lobbed a pass to Lexie in the hole set spot in front of the opposing goal. Lexie could have taken a shot but instead passed to Princess who fired in a blazer for about five yards out. For a group of 12-year-olds, it was very smooth.

"Yeah," Sandy smiled. "I have to admit I'm pleased. But the Raleigh teams haven't put up much of a struggle, and our girls still don't have the speed required to win at the national level."

"The national level? Is that what you're thinking about?" It was a question posed by Mrs. Scott. She and her husband had driven to Raleigh to watch their son's teams in action. "Yes," Sandy replied, turning to his mom and dad. "Why not?"

Mr. Scott supressed a laugh. "Ah, Sandy, my always-positive, always-hopeful son."

"Hey, folks," Sandy said with sudden seriousness. "If I could go to California and hold my own out there against some of the best players in the country, so can these kids." He turned back to the pool just as Cindy, the girl who'd joined the polo program in the springtime after advancing from the Y's swim classes, rose high out of the water with a strong egg-beater kick and intercepted a pass. "Look at that," Sandy shouted, pumping his fists. "You gotta believe."

* * * * *

The trip to Raleigh had been a success. They'd driven down the mountain through the early-morning fog and arrived in the state capital at noon, just in time to compete in the Saturday afternoon tournament. The vial of water from the Y pools back home had been dumped in the Sonner pool, and then the fun began. Raleigh had three teams of younger boys and two of even younger girls. They swam reasonably well but couldn't compare to Sandy's kids when it came to the basics of water polo. As Sabrina observed, "Too many coaches think that just because they have some fast swimmers, they can win at water polo. Not true. Obviously." Still, at the end of the afternoon of competition, Sandy & Co. gathered together and expressed appreciation to the president of the Triangle Water Polo Club for allowing the Western North Carolinians to participate. "Maybe you can bring one or two of your teams up the mountain to play in our pools next year."

The Scotts and the three other families that'd made the trip stayed overnight in Raleigh. Sandy took advantage of the situation to chat with some of the parents of his team members. They were generally supportive of his efforts but, as usual, wondered where the program was headed. With more than a little trepidation, the Head Lifeguard and Coach shared his vision of a move to national competition, which drew both positive and negative responses. After arising in mid-morning on Sunday and consuming a leisurely breakfast, they drove in their several cars past the capital building and then visited the Aquarium at Fort Fisher. "I feel a little guilty about skipping church," Mrs. Scott said. "Don't fret, Carrie," her husband consoled her. "Remember that wherever two or three are gathered in His name, the Spirit can be found. Today that applies to us and the other YMCA water polo families here."

Sandy nodded. "Yes indeed, it's the Y's way, a melding of the secular and the sacred."

* * * * *

The Lifeguard Games, held the weekend after the trip to Raleigh, were at least partially successful. Three dozen guards representing the Y's four aquatic operations participated. They had all received a list of events from Sandy in June. Some had spent time training, some had not. At the urging of his own crew, Sandy had taken part. "After all," Kristina said, "you ARE a working guard, aren't you?" Thus he turned over supervision of the event to his water polo assistant, Keith, and joined the list of competitors. "What if I don't finish in first place?" he asked his sister, Sabrina. "It'll just go to show you're human, like the rest of us," she said. "No one's perfect."

Sure enough, he failed to finish first. That honor was earned by a lifeguard from one of the other pools who was, Sandy admitted, very good. Chet, the young guard from the Downtown YMCA who'd been practicing diligently, was second. Sandy was third. He was delighted to see that Kristina placed in the top 10. "You've been practicing when I wasn't looking," he chided her. "Hey, big man," she retorted, "I can't let you be the only one around here who steals the show."

YMCA staff members Lydia and Tina, with whom he met a few days later, complimented him on both the Lifeguard Games and the successes of his young poloists. They'd invited Kirk, the head coach of the YMCA's youth swim squad, to join them in finalizing the autumn schedule. The two pools at the Downtown YMCA Aquatic Center and the larger pool at the Southside Y, where Kirk was stationed, were all closed for repairs, making this an ideal moment for the meeting. When it came time to discuss the water polo program, Sandy said, "As soon as we re-open, I'll need more pool time. It's as simple as that. We have 16 from the past school year who're still playing, and of the 12 who tried out in June, about half are good enough to continue."

Kirk, who also was fighting for pool time, had a recommendation. "Sandy, wouldn't it be better for your group to practice more often in a larger, deeper pool rather than in the small, shallow lap pool at the Downtown YMCA?" When Sandy nodded, Kirk went on. "We're okay with the Piranhas using the Downtown Y pool for our younger competitive swimmers. We don't necessarily need anything that's deeper, like you do. We have more than 30 signed up just in the 11 and 12s for the autumn season. That's a BUNCH to cram into the lap pool, but we'll manage. For your program, Sandy, I wonder if you can't somehow get the Y to pick up the cost of using the college pool for a second polo practice each week. You've attracted more players to your program who're bringing in more income, and you're still doing the coaching as an unpaid volunteer. The Y should reward you and your team."

It took a few weeks for Tina and Lydia to arrange for the Y to pay for the suggested second weekly practice at the college, during which time Sandy was negotiating with the college swim coach, but as September skimmed by, it appeared everything was set. "You've now been on board here for more than a year," Kristina said as she and Sandy sat on the bench that ran the length of the Downtown YMCA's lap pool. "I know you've signed up for a second year as the Head Lifeguard. Your job, your paying job, that is, seems to be going great. You've even squeezed a raise out of the YMCA, haven't you?"

"Yes and no. I told Lydia that I'd relinquish the raise if the Y would pay for our additional water polo practices at the college. That suggestion seemed to work out well for her budget."

"You're always a step ahead, aren't you? So, Sandyman, looking to the future, what's the plan?"

"With YMCA lifeguarding, or with water polo?"

"With the two of us."

CHAPTER TEN

HALLOWEEN SHOOTOUT

The meeting with the water polo parents was somewhat contentious, especially after Sandy presented his ambitious plan for the autumn months. He started by thanking the dozen parents in attendance for their support since the program was initiated by the YMCA the previous September. Then he reviewed all that had taken place, emphasizing the switch from Sandy Ball to *real* water polo, the game against the lifeguards, the one-day trip down the mountain, the weekend trip to the tournament in Philly, the enrollment of some new players, and the recent trip to Raleigh. He brought the group up to date on the autumn practice schedule. "We'll be returning to the 5:00 to 6:00 Tuesday and Thursday afternoon sessions at the Downtown YMCA, which will be used mainly – not entirely, but mainly – for swim conditioning. The kids will complain, I know they will, but it must be done. We'll be adding a Wednesday evening session at the college pool, 6:30 to 8:00 p.m., and we'll continue with the Saturday morning practices, 9:30 to 11:00 a.m. These will focus almost entirely on seven-per-side water polo."

There was a restlessness among the parents seated in the room, a murmuring, so Sandy hastened to add, "That's only five hours per week. Not much, to be honest. Most of the Y's swim team kids are practicing twice as much every week. Ten hours or more. If we, if you and your children, can't find five hours weekly for practicing, we might as well return to recreational Sandy Ball. If that's what you want, speak up."

He waited, looking around the room, but none of the moms or dads said a word. "Okay, then. I'd hoped we could qualify our girls' team for the national Rocktober tournament which is held every October. It's just for 12-and-unders. A big-time event that draws teams from coast to coast. But this now seems unlikely. We'd have to go to Florida for the Southeastern zone qualifying competition, and if we succeeded there, we'd have to travel all the way to Mesa, Arizona, for the Rocktober Championships. There's a team registration requirement, plus individual memberships, plus an entry fee that's excessive, plus the cost of flying to Florida, probably Orlando or Miami, and then, possibly, to Arizona. This doesn't include local or ground transportation, lodging, and meals ... well, the list goes on. It's simply more than we can afford. Much more. I'm sorry, because I believe our girls would do well."

"Is there an alternative?" one of the dads asked. "I'd like to see our team moving up the ladder, if at all possible."

With a smile, Sandy said, "I'm pleased to tell you there is indeed a very good alternative. The Colorado water polo people have a tournament named after Grier Laughlin, one of their former players and coaches who died several years ago in an unfortunate car accident. They've invited us to enter. It's being held in November, which is a perfect time for us. Like the Main Line tourney we attended in May, it's primarily for local teams but open to entries from elsewhere. In a way, it's a bigger event than the Rocktober as there are categories for 18-and-under, 15-and-under, 12-and-under, and 10-and-under. Lots of action. I know Albuquerque and Chicago have sent teams to the Colorado competition in the past, so it's an impressive event."

"Are there separate categories for boys and girls?" someone in the room asked.

"I don't think so. From what I can see, the 12-and-under competition is coed, or mixed. Whether that's good or bad for our gang, I'm not sure. But if you give me the go-ahead, I'll make inquiries and see if our kids can stay in the homes of the Colorado families. Like we did when we went to Philly. This would reduce the cost considerably. So ... wha'dya think."

There was a buzz as the parents discussed the matter amongst themselves. Sandy wasn't sure what to expect. He sat patiently, exchanging glances with Keith as they watched the parents weighing the pros and cons. Finally, one of the more vocal moms turned and said, "Go ahead, Sandy. We trust your judgment. You've done a good job so far with our youngsters, and we'd like you to continue exploring the possibility of entering the tournament in Colorado."

"Thanks. Now get up and stretch for a minute or so because I have two other items that shouldn't take much time."

It was five minutes before the parents settled down, at which time Sandy addressed them. "First, we don't have a team swim suit. The boys don't much care, but the girls do. With your permission, I'd like to work with the girls to select a suit. I'll try to keep the cost down. Do I have your approval?" Everyone in front of him nodded.

"Second, because it looks like you might be paying for another trip this year, this one to Colorado, I think we should have a couple of fund-raising activities. It would be cool for the kids to take responsibility for helping with the costs as much as they're able. We can conduct a swim-a-thon and also a car wash. Maybe some of you parents can hold a bake sale. I invite other ideas if you have them..."

This resulted in a 20-minute discussion before the meeting came to a close. By now Sandy knew most of the parents better than he did at the beginning of the polo program, so as they departed, he stood at the door and again expressed appreciation for their continuing support. "We're all in this together," he said. "It's strictly a team effort involving the kids, the coach, and the families." To himself he muttered, I believe it. I hope they do.

* * * * *

Practices were going well. What had started out a year ago as a recreational-type program that he called Sandy Ball had morphed into more of a competitive team, or teams. He now had 15 youngsters who'd been with him for a year or close to it, plus two who'd joined in the springtime from the Y's swim classes, plus half-a-dozen more who'd signed up for the summer months and shown some potential. One of the summer newcomers was a 12-year-old boy who had just moved to town. He'd been a star swimmer in his previous community. When Sandy tried to steer him to the Piranhas, his parents said they wanted him to try both activities, competitive swimming and water polo, and see which one he preferred. After Sandy saw him splashing up and down the pool, he'd immediately named him Tommy the Torpedo.

The Tuesday and Thursday late afternoon practices in the four-lane, shallow-end Downtown YMCA lap pool were now devoted almost entirely to swim-conditioning. At first the kids complained, but as they picked up the sport, they gradually became more enthused. Sandy didn't worry much, if at all, about starts and turns, and when doing sprints, he insisted the youngsters keep their heads raised high, water-polo style. He also worked a bit on the egg-beater kick, urging the team members to become more adept at playing "the vertical game."

The Wednesday evening and Saturday morning sessions at the six-lane, deep-water college pool were spent almost entirely on water polo. The makeshift college goals were put up, the balls tossed into the pool, and the caps distributed to the players. For the first 40 minutes, Sandy had his gang doing repetitive drills. "You can always improve your basic skills," he told his more experienced players, "and this will enable the newer team members to learn to dribble, pass, catch, and shoot." He then spent 15 or 20 minutes on defense. While his assistant, Keith, worked with the field players on maintaining position and using their hands discreetly, Sandy took his three goalies – Nona, Jose, newcomer Alden – to one end of the pool and taught them the special techniques of their position. In October, he had Janis join the goaltending group.

The practices always concluded with a scrimmage. While what he was doing was well-organized and sounded good, the simple fact was that these were 11- and 12-year-olds whose attention span was limited, along with their physical capabilities. When he told Kristina that "they just don't get it," she replied, "Oh, they get it, Sandy. They just can't do it ... yet. Be patient." To which he had to admit, "Patience is not my strong suite." To which she counseled him, saying, "But it's a mark of maturity."

When scrimmaging, he sometimes had the boys playing against the girls, while sometimes he divided the 22-member group into two or even three mixed, or coed, units. "If we go to Colorado, the 12-and-under competition there is for boys and girls combined. I'll have a really, REALLY tough time deciding on a team of 10 or 11 to take the trip. Our boys are getting bigger and better individually, especially with the addition of Tommy the Torpedo, but the girls have better teamwork. I know some of the kids are going to be disappointed if they're not chosen."

"And their parents, too," he was warned by Keith. "You'd better be ready for their comments."

"Gosh, there are times I wish I'd gone to California."

"No, you don't," Kristina chastised him.

"You're right," Sandy admitted. "I'm happy I'm here."

At the dinner table that same night, his mother asked, "What are you studying in your children's Sunday School class? I hear you talking about your lifeguarding job and water polo program, but I don't hear much about your church work. That's important, too, you know."

Sandy nodded. "I'm enjoying it more than I thought I would. There are seven or eight regulars in the class, plus two or three others who attend occasionally. We've been studying the Beatitudes. I've been trying to move on to something else, but the kids keep posing one question after another, week after week. I'm learning a lot myself by teaching them."

"That's the way it goes with teaching," his dad said.

"So what have you decided about the poor being blessed?" Sabrina wanted to know. "Or is it the poor in spirit?" And off they went on a lengthy family discussion that kept them gathered around the table for nearly an hour.

The next day, one of the most experienced of the YMCA lifeguards informed Sandy that he was resigning. "Oh, no," Sandy put his hands to his head. "You're one of our best, Melvin. What's the problem?"

"I like working for the YMCA. I like working with you. I just need to earn more money. The lifeguards aren't paid enough. Some part-time Y employees who don't have half as much responsibility as we do are earning a dollar per hour more. Over a week, a month, a year, that adds up. I've accepted a position elsewhere. So this is my two-week notice. Sorry. But I believe two or three other guards feel the same way I do."

Soon thereafter, Sandy met with Lydia, the Director of Aquatics, and pleaded his case. "Can't we pay the guards more?"

"I wish we could. After all, I used to guard here myself, so I can sympathize. But my department, like the others, has a tight budget. We can't spend what we don't have. We bring in money through memberships, classes, donations, special programs like yours, and various other sources. Then we figure out what we can spend. It's that simple. Except that it's really not simple at all. Most of us devote more hours than you realize to balancing our budgets."

"So if we brought in more income, we could spend more for … whatever."

"That's the way it works. Aren't you meeting occasionally with the former Director of Aquatics who was also the swimming and water polo coach?"

"We're having a monthly lunch meeting."

"Well, when I took this job, I also had a meeting with him. He gave me some excellent advice, and I particularly remember one thing he said. It was this: no program is successful until it's paid for."

Sandy ended up dreaming about it. Money for operating the Aquatic Center which included water, chemicals, heating, electricity. Money for full-time and part-time staff. Money for more equipment than imaginable that had to be constantly repaired or replaced. Money for insurance coverage and such behind-the-scenes necessities. When it came to Sandy's water polo program, money for renting the college pool for the second (additional) weekly practice on Wednesday evenings. And yes, money for taking trips.

Thus it was on a Saturday afternoon following the normal practice at the college pool that Sandy and his troops gathered at a neighborhood gas station and conducted a car wash. They'd done a decent job of advertising, and with the weather cooperating, the cars were lined up. The kids spent four hours giving every vehicle a thorough cleansing. When it was over, Kristina, who's been collecting money from the motorists, said, "We've earned $280. Is that good or bad?"

"I have no idea," Sandy replied, "but it was a worthwhile bonding experience for the team members and should give them some satisfaction for helping with our expenses."

On Columbus Day, the Downtown YMCA closed a few hours earlier than usual, and Sandy arranged for the water poloists to use the pool after the general membership had departed. It was for a swim-a-thon, another fund-raising effort, and the team brought in $400. "Every little bit helps," Keith told them.

Then one night when he was at home, his dad shouted, "There's a phone call for you, son."

When Sandy lifted the receiver, he discovered that the caller was Champ, the former YMCA swimming and water polo coach. After exchanging pleasantries, Champ said, "We hear you're hoping to take your team on a trip to Colorado. Is that right?"

"Yep, that's the plan, if we can work it out."

"Well, as you know, Sandy, we have a YMCA Water Polo Alumni Club comprised of about 40 players from the 1970s and 1980s. I'm in touch with them frequently via email, and we meet for lunch from time to time. It's a great group. They contribute to the Y's campaign each year, and they helped pay the publishing costs for my last book, *Water Polo the Y's Way*. They appreciate your efforts to revive the sport here, and they know that you're doing it free of charge. So they've decided to pay your way to Colorado. Just let me know how much it'll be."

Stunned, all Sandy could say was, "WOW!"

* * * * *

A second phone call also caught Sandy by surprise. It was the coach of the team from down the mountain, against whom they'd played a few months previously, calling to seek a rematch "either in our pool or yours." Sandy replied, "Let's do it here in two weeks, provided I can get the college pool so we can play seven-per-side."

The local newspaper learned of the event and called it the Halloween Shootout, posting an article that said, "High-level water polo returns to the mountains after a lengthy absence. The YMCA once fielded teams that won national titles, some of them in tourneys held here and some in pools scattered across the country. While the sport has continued to be played locally on a recreational basis, the last national event occurred in 1984, when an Olympic Development Clinic featuring silver medalist Joe

Vargas from California attracted a sizeable turnout from several of our mountains communities.

"Now two national stars from California will be competing against each other on Halloween weekend. One is Sandy Scott, a local lad who played four years of collegiate water polo at Golden Gate Community College and Western California University, earning All-America honors. He trained at the national water polo center in Los Alamitos before returning home. He'll be representing the home team against the visitors who will be led by Travis Tucker, a talented Californian who recently moved to the Carolinas. The Masters game is scheduled for 1 p.m. at the college pool and will be followed by a junior boys' game and a junior girls' contest.

"The two local junior teams are being coached by Scott at the YMCA. So far this year they've participated in tournaments in Philadelphia and Raleigh, and Scott has entered them in a mid-November tourney in Thornton, Colorado."

In return for convincing the college swim coach to let him use the pool for the forthcoming competition, Sandy had agreed to replace the flimsy, makeshift inner-tube water polo goals with official and more substantial cages. At home one night, he told his family members, "The ol' coach told me that when he was playing and coaching in the 1960s and 1970s, both in the Midwest and here, they never bought a single goal. Couldn't afford it. They built all the goals locally. For the college pool we're using, in which they also practiced and played, they bought lumber, and he and his young players spent a weekend hammering together wooden goals for each end of the pool. As always, they fitted the goals with used soccer netting. They lasted for 10 years, he said, and teams came from far and wide to compete here and never complained. So that's what we'll do."

When he shared the plan with his young players, they weren't exactly enthused. Ellery, outspoken as usual, said, "Promoting and coaching and playing water polo around here isn't easy, is it?"

"No," Sandy agreed, "and it's always been that way. But it's worth doing. I'll purchase the materials we need, and y'all see if you can find some used or discarded soccer netting."

It took the entire following weekend to complete the task, but with the two goals, or cages, having been built, a laborious process, the Masters adult team and YMCA youth teams were ready for action. Sandy remained in reasonably good shape, thanks to the lifesaving training and swimming he was doing at the Y, although his water polo skills were a little rusty. Several hundred spectators were gathered alongside the college pool when the teams from down the hill arrived.

The visitors had bulked up their Masters team with a couple of new players, including Travis Tucker, the ringer from California. Like Sandy, he was big, strong, and swift. When the game commenced, the two of them took it to each other. Up and down the pool they battled, above the surface and below, as the referee, provided by the visiting team, seemed reluctant to call any fouls. They grabbed and grappled for the full four quarters. When it was over, Travis turned to Sandy and said, "That was wonderful."

Sandy, smiling as he and his opponent embraced in the water, replied, "It surely was. You brought out the best in me. By the way, what was the final score?"

"I have no idea."

The junior games were supposedly for those 14 and younger. No one bothered checking any birth certificates, so Sandy told his boys, who were being coached by Keith, that they should keep their heads up, toughen up, and play smart. "Their boys were faster than our team when we went to their pool, but with the swim-conditioning you've been doing, you should be able to keep up with them. I know you can guard better. So go get' em."

It was a close encounter. Like Sandy's squad, the visiting boys were definitely improved. But with the addition of Tommy the Torpedo to the starting lineup of Jose, Ben, Junior, Ellery, Warner, and Hector, and with Alden, Leland, Clayton, and Jack serving as subs, the home team won out by a narrow two-goal margin. Keith, who'd worn himself out shouting from the sidelines, was jubilant. "You guys did it!"

The girls' game was not so closely contested. The visitors, like far too many water polo programs, appeared to have treated the ladies as an after-thought. The men and boys were important. Not so the young girls, who weren't pushed hard enough to excel. Sandy's starting lineup of Nona, Delia, Savannah, Wanda, Princess, Janis, and Lexie was clearly superior and bolted to a 3-to-0 advantage. In the second round of the four-quarter clash, Sandy experimented, letting Janis play goalie and putting subs Beatrice, Cindy, and summer newcomers Erin and Missy into the fray. He still had Delia in the pool on defense and Lexie as hole set. He told Delia, "Get the ball to Lexie." She did, and Lexie added two goals to the one she'd scored in the opening period.

During the third and fourth quarters, the girls continued to dominate, with everyone contributing, and the final score favored the YMCA team, 13-to-3.

Most of the Masters players had departed, not bothering to stick around for the junior games, but after the Y youngsters has showered and changed and gathered with their parents on the deck, Sandy addressed them all. "This is a proud moment for our program. It's not just that our boys and girls won. It's always nice to win. That's why we keep score. But it's important to do it the right way, the Y's way, which we've done. As I've repeatedly emphasized, this is a total team effort. The kids practice hard and do their best. I coach and do my best, with Keith's assistance. And you, the parents, provide the funding and the encouragement. I'm gratified, and I hope you are, too. I suggest you spend the rest of the weekend celebrating Halloween, if you wish, or just relaxing. Then we need to get ready for our next challenge, which is the trip to Colorado in two weeks."

The bad news arrived the following day in yet another phone call to the Scott household. "It's for you, once again," Sabrina told her brother.

"Hello, this is Sandy."

"This is Delia's dad. I want you to know Delia and her brother, Harold, have been in a car accident. He's in the hospital. It doesn't look good. Delia is shaken but seems to be okay. I'll keep you posted." The phone clicked off.

Chapter Eleven

COLORADO COOL

"It wasn't as hard as I thought it'd be," Sandy said as he and Kristina sat on the familiar riverside bench on a cool autumn afternoon.

"What wasn't?"

"Two things. First was replacing Melvin in our lifeguarding crew. When I advertised, we had a dozen applicants. I narrowed the choices to three, interviewed each one, and made my pick. It was Vic, whom you met the other day. He isn't as experienced as Melvin, but he has a pleasant personality and seems to have good potential. I think, I hope, he'll work out."

"I have to say he's a cutie," Kristina smiled, "and he's not married, but he's a little old for me."

"Old? He's only 28. What's old about that?"

"My upper age range is 25. By the way, isn't that *your* age, Sandy?"

It was the Head Lifeguard's turn to chuckle. "Okay, I know when you're teasing me."

"So what else was easier to do than you expected?"

"Selecting the players to go to Colorado. With a roster of more than 20, I was worried I'd cause hurt feelings and upset parents. But everything fell into place. According to the rules, we're allowed to take 13 players and two coaches. That worked out perfectly for us. Since this is a 12-and-under competition, Hector, at 14, almost 15, is definitely too old. Ben and Savannah have had birthdays and are now 13. It'll be difficult to leave them at home, but I have no other option. Several of the newcomers are simply not ready. So that leaves ..."

He stopped and began counting on his fingers ... "Lexie, Princess, Nona, Janis, Beatrice, Wanda, Warner, Jose, Ellery, Junior, Clayton ... is that 10 or 11? Who am I forgetting?"

"It's 11, and it's obvious you didn't major in math. You didn't mention two of your best players, Delia and Tom."

"Ah, yes, how could I forget Tommy the Torpedo! What a great addition to our team he is. And we'll be depending more than ever on Delia since Savannah's aged up."

"What's the story on Delia's brother?"

"He's still in the hospital. I'm told he's had seven or eight surgeries, but it looks like he'll make it. Delia suffered some scrapes and bruises and still has a bump on her forehead. She was shaken up but seems to be all right now. She's missed the last two Tuesday and Thursday swim-conditioning practices at the Y because she's gone to the hospital to check on Harold, but the doc and her parents have given her permission to take the trip. As you know, her mom has insisted on going along with her, so I've put her down as the assistant coach or chaperone. Sorry, Kristina. I was hoping you could go."

"No problem, Sandstorm the Great. I don't mind. You've listed all 13 players. What're your chances?"

"I think if we were playing our girls against other girls at either tournament, the one in Arizona or the one in Colorado, we'd have a chance to take top honors. Well, that's not completely true. I'm sure we'd meet their match, and then some, when we played the Californians. They'd most likely sock it to us. And yet, our girls are good, even without Savannah.

"But in a coed or mixed tourney, such as the one last spring in Pennsylvania and the one coming up in Colorado, I don't think our boys can hold their own. They're just not quite ... how should I put it ... ready for major competition. So what are our chances, you ask? Time will tell, as Champ, the former YMCA swimming and water polo coach, likes to say."

* * * * *

Money. There was that word again. Seated around the family dinner table, Sandy was counting his water polo pennies, so to speak. "Let's see. We've raised $280 from the car wash and $400 from the swim-a-thon. The parents brought in about $225 from their bake sale. Thanks to Champ, the YMCA's Alumni Water Polo Club members have donated another $650."

"But that's money they gave to you, Sandy," his sister insisted, "to cover your travel expenses to Colorado."

"Maybe so, but I'm tossing it into the team's treasury. I believe it adds up to approximately $1,500."

"Not a lot," Mr. Scott observed. "Not much at all," Mrs. Scott contributed.

"No," Sandy admitted, "but thankfully, the Y's board of directors has again consented to pay the entry fee for the tourney, which is $350. Some of the older board members were around when the Y had its championship water polo teams in the past, and I know they're delighted to see the polo program being revived."

"So what's your plan moneywise?" asked Sandy's grandfather, sitting in a corner of the room.

"We have $1,500, and with 15 of us making the trip – 13 players, one parent, and myself – that'll be $100 that we can give to each person. Should cover their meals and personal, incidental expenses."

"Not a lot," Mr. Scott observed again. "Not much at all," Mrs. Scott repeated.

"It'll have to do. We've finally paid all that we owed for our trips to Philly and Raleigh, so now we only have to pay for the Colorado trip. Somehow."

"Put it on your credit card, Sandy, just as you did before," Sabrina stated.

"I've already done so. I'm embarrassed to tell you how much. After spending umpteen hours or days, actually, looking at our various options, I've booked a travel package for us that includes round-trip air fare, airport shuttle service from Denver to the suburb of Thornton and back again, and a motel that will let us squeeze three or four to a room for three nights and will provide us with a free breakfast each morning. It wasn't working out for us to stay in the homes of the host organization, and I decided I wanted our team to remain together, anyway. So … it figures out to roughly $500 per person. That's not bad."

"You've put it on your credit card?" Sandy's grandmother asked incredulously.

"Half the families are reimbursing me up front. The other half, with a single exception, will be repaying me one month at a time. It's the best we can do."

As silence filled the room, with each member of the Scott family lost in his or her own thoughts, Sandy felt a need to say more. "Look, this is a Y program we're talking about. It's for Y members, most of whom are the hoi polloi we talked about last year. Average folks, with a limited income. This family should certainly understand what that means. We just can't give up and hide in our little corner of the world. We must do what we can to give the kids in our Y programs the best experiences possible."

The conversation continued for another half-hour before Sandy brought it to a conclusion. "Money, or the lack of it, isn't our only problem. We lost two weeks of swim-conditioning time when the pools were closed for repair. Two of our best players, Ben and Savannah, have aged up and can't go with us to the Grier Laughlin tournament. Delia was in a car accident. We're running short on equipment. I had a phone call the other night from a mom who's disappointed her son hasn't been selected for the trip."

"Only one parent who's voiced a complaint? You're lucky."

"Well, you know what they say. Adversity builds character. Without adversity, we could never mature and face up to all the things in life."

"What things?"

"More adversity."

* * * * *

When they arrived at the Denver International Airport, it was noon on Friday. And snowing. Not hard, but enough to make the streets slippery. "Stick close," Sandy shouted as the 13 youngsters and two adults tried to locate the departure gate for the shuttle service to the nearby community of Thornton. It took the better part of an hour for them to find the shuttle and cram inside, where they sat shoulder to shoulder with the other passengers. After winding through slushy streets and making several stops, the shuttle reached the YMCA team's destination.

It was a motel into which they crowded, reminding Sandy of the story about the Pied Piper and his followers. Checking in and obtaining keys to their five rooms, the Y coach said, "We're on the second floor. Let's walk up the stairs. Don't forget your luggage. You know who your roommates are, so when you get to your rooms, lie down and rest for an hour. That's an order."

He checked his list. Beatrice, Wanda, Princess, and Janis together. Lexie, Nona, Delia, and the chaperoning mom together. Ellery, Jose, and Clayton together. Warner, Junior, and Tommy together. Who else? Oh, yes, himself, who was occupying his own room, the one perk he was allowing himself. It was conveniently placed between the two rooms shared by the six boys, hopefully to keep them separated and reasonably peaceful. I'm ready for a one-hour nap myself, he realized.

It wasn't exactly a surprise, but nonetheless it took their breath away. Back home, Sandy has shown his kids the web-site for the Veterans Memorial Aquatic Center in Thornton where the water polo tournament was to be conducted. It had been completed in 2010 at a cost of nearly $20 million and was one of the finest indoor aquatic complexes – three pools altogether, with seating for over 800 spectators – in the country. "Whew," outspoken Ellery whispered as the Western North Carolina contingent walked into the mammoth facility on Friday evening, shaking snow from their clothing. "Seeing a picture of it on the computer screen is NOTHING compared to actually being here, in person."

Lexie, usually so soft-spoken, agreed, saying, "You could fit four or five of our Y pools into this area." "And have space left over," Warner added.

"Now you know why I had you working on your long passes, those of 10 or 15 yards," Sandy said as he followed his usual procedure and emptied the vial of water taken from the YMCA Aquatic Center pool back home into the gigantic Veterans Memorial pool. "The goalies have to pass out to mid-pool to get their team's offense started, and the field players have to make crisp cross-pool passes and … well … you hear what I'm saying. A team that passes accurately on offense and displays a strong defense will usually beat a team that merely swims fast."

"Yeah, yeah, yeah," several youngsters chimed in at the same time. "We know what you always tell us, Coach. How fast can an opposing player swim if you're holding on to him?"

"Holding on to an opponent?" Sandy shrugged innocently. "Surely I've never taught you that." Everyone laughed.

They weren't laughing, however, an hour later when the halftime score of their opening game showed them trailing, 5-to-3. Talking calmly at poolside, Sandy said, "This is a team you can beat. Their lineup is half boys and half girls, just like ours. They don't swim any faster. They may have played in more tourneys, more games, than you have, but that doesn't mean anything. You have two quarters to put it together. They're guarding Lexie closely, but I don't think they can stop her IF we can get the ball to her. Delia, you need to take a shot or two. You're doing great on defense, but we need to score more. Same with you, Tommy. You're the Torpedo, remember? Get goin'. Don't be scared to shoot. The rest of you, tighten up on defense. Don't give up any easy goals. Use your arms, hands, legs. Toughen up."

Tommy sprinted for the ball as the third period started, captured it easily, and passed to Delia. She dribbled down the pool and passed to Lexie in the hole set spot. Lexie faked left, faked right, and then, surprisingly, passed to a wide-open Princess, who with her strong arm powered in a shot. "Way to go!" Sandy shouted.

Now the test would come. The Y team had its best offensive players in the water, and without Ben, their best guard who'd aged up and hadn't made the trip, they were weaker defensively. Could they stop the opposing team from Albuquerque? The answer was no. The well-coached New Mexico kids advanced the ball into scoring territory, and although their passing was suspect, they scored.

"Move it, move it," Sandy instructed as his team went on offense again. They did start moving faster, and after a few passes, the ball went into Lexie. This time, with no wasted effort, she jabbed her opponent aside and popped a shot into the corner of the cage. Once again the 'querque kids' advanced the ball down the pool and somehow managed to take a shot. Jose, who was playing goalie, leapt high and made the stop. "To Tommy, pass to Tommy," Sandy yelled, and when Tommy received the ball, Sandy yelled again, "Turn on the steam." That's what Tommy did, dribbling quickly toward the opposing cage. He was in the clear, no one near him, but he hesitated. "Swim ... shoot!" the Y subs shouted from sidelines, and Tommy took a couple of strokes forward and then scored from the four-yard line.

That's how the third quarter ended, with the teams tied, 6-to-6. "Listen," Sandy told the Y youngsters, "this is what I want you to do. For the first few minutes of the final period, you'll play strictly defense. Don't worry about scoring. If you get a shot from in front of their goal, take it, but otherwise, concentrate on defense. Stay back, for the most part. Do good egg-beater kicking to stay high in the water. Hands up. Don't let your opponent get around you. When there's about two minutes to go and we have possession, you'll hear me shout. Then, go for it. Everybody sprint down the pool. Delia, you control the ball. Take it down the middle. Everyone spread out and become a scoring threat. Pass it around. If you have a clear shot, Princess, take it from outside. If we're running out of time, pass into Lexie. Then, Lexie, it's up to you."

Later, alone in his motel room, Sandy reflected on what had happened. His team had followed his instructions almost to the letter. They were aggressive on defense for several minutes, turning back the New Mexico offense, and with less than two minutes remaining and Ellery having stolen the ball, Sandy shouted, "Now!" The six YMCA field players sprinted toward the opposing goal. Delia dribbled, passed to Tommy, who passed to Princess, who fumbled the ball. She picked it up and almost shot from six yards out. Almost. Instead she passed to Lexie who, as always, jostled aside her defender and swept the ball toward the corner of the cage. The defending goalie stuck out his arm and blocked the shot. "Oh, no!" Sandy muttered. The ball bounced right back to Lexie, who took a second shot. Score! "Oh, yeah," Sandy exhaled. Then, "Defense! Defense!" Albuquerque had possession one more time but didn't get off a shot. When the whistle sounded, ending the game, it was 7-to-6 in favor of the Sandy Ballers.

* * * * *

At breakfast the next morning, Sandy gathered his team together. "We didn't talk much last night, but I want to repeat what I said then. You showed a lot of courage and determination, coming back in the second half to win. That was a good group of kids you beat. Why did we win? First, because you tightened up on defense. Second, because you swam harder when we had the ball. That opened up some shots for us. The swim-conditioning we've been doing back home definitely paid off last night. Don't eat too much this morning. We have a game at 10 a.m. against another strong squad. And bundle up when we go outside. Put on your sweatshirts and jackets. It's still snowing a little."

The morning game was against a good Colorado team named the Neptunes. It was a back-and-forth battle with the lead changing hands from quarter to quarter. Since the subs hadn't played much the night before, Sandy kept them in the game longer than usual, hoping that his starters, when inserted in the fourth quarter, could pull it out. Unfortunately, they didn't perform as well as they had against Albuquerque, and the result was a deadlock, 8-to-8. Because there were numerous other games to be played in the older age categories, the tie stood.

The 4 p.m. contest was against a team from Missouri. When Sandy initially learned the Y kids would be facing such an opponent, he was worried. St. Louis had a 100-year-old history of water polo involvement, and nowadays their teams were among the nation's best at every level. Then he realized that the top St. Louis teams – Clayton, Daisy, Jungle Cat, Mad Dog – were probably busy with the Junior Olympics and Rocktober and other such national events. So who was coming to the Grier Laughlin tourney? It turned out to be a young team from one of the Sr. Louis suburbs. They'd been playing summer polo at an outdoor pool, mostly recreational, and the kids had enjoyed it so much they wanted to keep playing after school started. The trip to Colorado was "for fun," their coach said, and "a learning experience."

Sandy's squad was older and more experienced and better, and after his starters rang up an 8-to-2 halftime lead, he was able to use the subs in the second half. The final score favored the Western North Carolinians by 12-to-6. Lexie had fired in four goals before retiring to the bench, and five other players tallied once or twice. "It was like a scrimmage," stated Junior, who replaced Lexie as hole set in the third and fourth quarters. "Don't get cocky," his coach reprimanded him. "Remember that one of our Y values is about being respectful. This applies to our opponents in water polo. Besides, they're a young team of mostly 11-year-olds. If they keep practicing and return to this tourney next year, they'll do much better."

Sandy ate dinner that evening with Crazy Dave, who was coach of the Wyoming team against whom the Western North Carolina kids would be playing on Sunday morning. The two teams were staying in the same motel and had begun mingling with each other. Dave had grown up in Niagara Falls, where his dad was a well-known swimming and water polo coach. "I got my nickname, Crazy Dave, when I was just a boy, growing up and doing some silly things," the Wyoming coach said, "like so many other boys." He smiled and added, "I prefer to be called Coach Dave now."

"You never tried to go over Niagara Falls, did you?" Sandy inquired, taking a bite of steak.

"No, I never contemplated it. I may have acted a bit crazy, but I've never been stupid. I was a decent swimmer and polo player and ended up coming out West for college, to my dad's alma mater at the University of Wyoming, where I continued to play polo. Our men's team was mediocre, but I averaged nearly 10 goals per game at the hole set position. After getting married, settling down in Wyoming, and working at a full-time job, I served in my spare time as a radio commentator and writer about the sport for the Water Polo Planet organization. It was fun, but the gig finally ended. Thus in the past year I've assembled a youth team, which is the one I've brought to the Grier Laughlin tourney. It's a group of fast-swimming youngsters who're still learning the fundamentals of water polo. So far we've been beaten by Albuquerque and the two Colorado clubs. I doubt we'll provide much opposition for your team tomorrow morning. Your gang does well for a bunch of 12-year-olds, and your girl who plays hole set is exceptional."

"Yes," Sandy agreed. "She's tall and tough, and she can really shoot, and although no one notices, she covers well on defense. Our hometown newspaper recently did a series on local sports stars of the future. They mentioned the usual young standouts in football, basketball, baseball, soccer, and other sports, and at the end of the series, they added water polo. They called Lexie a Water Polo Whiz with a bright future. I'd say that's putting it mildly. She turns 13 in two weeks, on Thanksgiving Weekend, which is when I also have my birthday. But enough on that subject. Who else do you play tomorrow?"

Coach Dave took a swig of his drink and buttered a roll before answering. "We have one final game tomorrow afternoon against the Missouri kids, and maybe we can win that one. But it's all right. We're here to learn and have a good time."

Just then Sandy's cell phone rang. It was Kristina, calling from back home and wanting to know how the team had done in its two Saturday matches. They talked so long that Crazy Dave eventually waved and walked away. "See you in the pool tomorrow morning."

When the games were scheduled to start early on Sunday, the referees hadn't shown up. They've been delayed by the wintry weather, someone said. Sandy had his team sit on the sidelines and relax and watch the older players in the 18-and-under and 15-and-under age categories warm-up. He pointed out some things they were doing right and some they were doing wrong, but it was obvious his kids weren't paying attention. They were chatting amongst themselves and with their newfound friends from Wyoming and playing their hand-held computer games. Having played three games so far without a loss – defeating Albuquerque and the entry from suburban St. Louis and tying one of the hometown teams – the Y youngsters seemed confident. How could they lose to these beginners from Wyoming?

Coach Dave was the reason they could lose. He certainly wasn't crazy, Sandy realized after the refs arrived and the games started and, finally, at 11 a.m., it was time for the matchup between the two 12-and-under teams. Boasting plenty of speed but not much in the way of water polo skills, the Wyoming kids focused on defense. They gathered in a zone formation in front of their cage, treading and holding their hands high. Whenever the Y team tossed the ball to Lexie in the hole, the westerners collapsed on her and prevented her from shooting. When they had possession, they sent just one player speeding as swiftly as possible down the pool. Figuring this one player could spring free for a shot, they threw him, or her, a long pass and hoped for the best. The remainder of the team stayed back on defense. Luckily Sandy had Tommy the Torpedo on whom to rely. This recent addition to his Y team was able to keep up with the Wyoming swifties on their one-on-one moves.

That Dave is a wily coach, Sandy said to himself in admiration at halftime, with his kids holding a slim 3-to-2 lead. Lexie had escaped the clutches of her defenders to pop in one shot. She'd also drawn a kick-out foul, and taking advantage of the extra-man situation, Princess had scored from the outside. The third tally was tossed in by Warner on a lucky lob.

"Let's do this," Sandy told his troops. "Junior, I want you to play hole set. If somehow the ball gets to you and you're free, take a shot. But don't try too hard. You're mainly a decoy. Lexie, I want you to move outside on the left wing. Ellery, you're here, and Princess, you're in the middle, and Warner, you're over here on the right side. Pass the ball around two or three times, and whichever one of you gets a good look, shoot. Fire away. Aim high for the corners. Tommy, you're continuing to play defense. Hang back, and if Wyoming realizes they can't get a swimmer past you, it'll be interesting to see how they'll react. The only time I want you to join the offense is when, and if, we have an extra-man. Jose, you're in as goalie. Be alert. Everyone got it? Okay, let's play ball."

The third quarter wasn't pretty. The Y youngsters were trying something new on offense, while the Wyoming kids found their offense being thwarted. Sandy and Coach Dave smiled at each other as they saw their respective teams struggling. Gradually, the Western North Carolinians pulled away. Warner scored on another lob, which the Wyoming goalie seemed unable to detect as the ball flew over his head. When Junior drew a exclusion, Princess threatened to shoot from the outside, waving the ball back and forth in the air. Then she passed to Lexie, who caught the ball on the left side and in one quick motion powered a shot into the opposite corner of the cage. As the period ended, Sandy & Co. had extended their lead to 5-to-2.

"Same thing for the final five minutes," Sandy said, "except that you're back in the game, Delia, replacing Princess. On offense, pass the ball around the perimeter, like you've been doing, but don't be too eager to shoot. Be patient. Defense is the name of the game now. Cover closely. Press. Be aggressive. Hands up. These kids" – he pointed to the Wyoming team gathered around Coach Dave across the pool – "are swimmers, not water poloists. Show 'em what *real* water polo feels like … under the surface. You know what I mean, what I always tell you." The Y kids laughed.

The fourth quarter unfolded as planned, and Sandy eventually found himself relaxing. Delia raced out to gain control of the ball in mid-pool at the start. She passed to Tommy, who passed back to her, and as she so often did, she dribbled down the pool and, before the westerners could set up their defense, she reared back and hit from four yards out.

Then some sloppy defensive play resulted in Ellery being excluded for 30 seconds. Coach Dave called a timeout and told his team what to do with their extra-man advantage. They responded by passing and dropping the ball and passing and dropping the ball and then, in a skirmish in front of the YMCA team's cage, the ball was somehow, by someone, batted in.

Once again on offense, the Y players did as instructed, with Junior sitting in the hole and the others passing back and forth around the perimeter. When Lexie received the ball, she repeated her previous performance, catching the pass and shooting in a single movement and putting a blazer in the opposite corner of the Wyoming cage.

With two minutes to go, Coach Dave sent in his subs, and Sandy called a timeout and did likewise. "Nona, grab the red cap from Jose. Wanda and Warner, you're in. So are you, Beatrice and Clayton and Janis." To those in the water, who'd been playing, he said, "Everyone out except Delia. You stay in … you're the quarterback."

When it was over and the teams lined up and shook hands with each other, Coach Dave said to Sandy, "Hey, we didn't do too badly, did we? I thought we'd lose by at least 10. Instead it was just four."

"Your coaching kept it close," Sandy stated "Good luck this afternoon against the Missouri team."

"Good luck to YOU this afternoon against the Pirates, the top Colorado youth team. I hear they went out to California not so long ago and whipped all of the 12-and-unders out there."

"Oh, no, did you have to tell me?"

* * * * *

The less said about our last game, the better, thought Sandy, as he sat in the Denver International Airport with Delia and her mother, who'd been serving as chaperone. The hometown Pirates had defeated the team from Western North Carolina by a four-goal margin. Earlier in the year, the Pirates had traveled to California and won the prestigious Winterfest Championships with a record of five victories and only one loss. They were as good as the top 12-and-under teams in the Philly tourney, if not better, Sandy surmised, and apparently superior to most of the California clubs they'd played.

Still, they're not four goals better than my team! We simply didn't play well, the YMCA coach acknowledged when the game was over … and again later on when he was sitting in his motel room and reviewing what had happened. The Pirates were playing in a familiar pool; they were sleeping in their own beds and eating properly; they probably didn't have to slush through the snow each day, getting lost in the process (like our kids, Sandy remembered, shaking his head dejectedly); they were fresh. What else? Quit making excuses, he told himself. The Pirates were better. But not by four goals!

Turning to Delia's mom, he said, "Thanks again for coming along. We couldn't have done it without you, and that's the truth. I know how very hard it must have been for you to leave your son in the hospital back home, but from every report, Harold is recovering."

"Yes," the lovely lady replied in her soft voice. "I've been calling home every morning and evening to check in, and my husband says it's going well. I'm glad I came, and I'm so proud of Delia and her teammates. They did well, don't you think?"

Delia, seated between her mom and her coach, lifted the large trophy. "This'll be *something* to show everyone when we get home."

Sandy nodded just as he felt a tingling in his pocket. "My phone," he blurted. It was his sister, Sabrina. "How's the weather in Denver?" she asked.

"It's snowing harder than ever," Sandy informed her. "After we lost our last game Sunday afternoon, we barely made it back to the motel. Luckily there's a nice steak house next door, so we didn't have to go far for our meals. The kids were tired. So was I. We hit the sack early, planning to go sight-seeing when we awakened before catching the flight home today. No such luck. The snow was continuing."

"So what'd you do?"

"Believe it or not, the motel has an indoor pool, which is one reason I booked us there. Our youngsters and their new friends from Wyoming spent this morning splashin' around. You'd think they'd had enough of it after playing five games in three days, but this was different. No one was trying to beat anyone else. It was a bunch of kids from East and West enjoying their childhood. Then we hopped on the shuttle which made its way to the airport through the snow drifts … and here we are … awaiting our flight."

"Well, Sandy," said Sabrina, "you need to know that the storm has reached us, too. It's started snowing in Atlanta and is moving in our direction. Supposed to hit the mountains in two or three hours. Y'all may make it home, or you may not. Be prepared. They're already announcing the cancellation of some flights."

"Not to worry, sister dear. You remember what I told the family the other night? Adversity builds character, and without character, a person could never mature and face up to all the things in life … such as more adversity. So cheer up."

"Hey, big brother, who's forever the optimist, just remember how you feel about adversity and how it builds character when you and the kids are sleeping on the floor of an airport somewhere tonight."

Chapter Twelve

TEAM SPIRIT

"How about Sandy's Saints?" suggested Ben.

"Are you kidding?" replied Savannah. "There's nothing saintly about you boys."

"How about Sandy's Sugar-coated Sissies? That's you girls." So said Clayton.

"How 'bout we name your boys' team the Frog Faces?" sneered Beatrice.

"Now be nice," intervened Sabrina. "There's no need to mention Sandy at all. Just pick out a name that appeals to most of the team members."

A dozen of the Y water poloists had gathered to choose a nickname. Sandy had decided to stay away from the meeting, permitting the kids to make their own decision, but had sent his sister to supervise the process. It had all started when the team was waiting in a darkened corner of the Charlotte airport on their return home from the Grier Laughlin tourney in Colorado. Home? Not that night. Their flight from Denver to Charlotte was an hour late in departing due to the wintry weather and arrived in Charlotte too late to connect with the usual late-night commuter flight to the mountains of Western North Carolina. When Sandy and the kids called their parents, they were all informed that no flights were being allowed to land, anyway. Sandy's sister chided him in an I-told-you-so voice. "Enjoy your character-building night in the airport."

So there they were, or had been, in the Charlotte airport, with nowhere to go. Before sinking into an exhausted sleep around 2 a.m., the youngsters had discussed a subject brought up by Janis.

She said, "We need a nickname. The swim squad back home is the Piranhas. The teams we just played all had names. The two Colorado clubs were the Pirates and the Neptunes. The Albuquerque team that wore red, white, and blue suits called themselves the Stars and Stripes. The Missouri team was the Mighty Dinos. The Wyoming team was the Little Camels."

"We can come up with a better name than any of those!" exclaimed Beatrice.

"Tell you what," Sandy said in weary exasperation. "Let's all go to sleep and dream about it. They say that much of what we do creatively comes out of our dreams. It's when our sub-conscious takes over and … well … just go to sleep."

Which, amazingly, the youngsters did, and the next morning they were able to board a flight and return to their hometown airport, where the runways had been cleared. It was still snowing slightly, but almost all of the parents were there to greet them, some having taken off from work to do so.

Now, two weeks later, it was Thanksgiving Weekend, and as he'd done the year before, Sandy set up a special program for Saturday. He invited the parents to attend. First there was the meeting to select a team nickname. This was followed by an exhibition scrimmage in the small Y pool with the kids divided into three somewhat evenly-matched teams. Whereas the game one year ago had been Sandy Ball with limited contact, designed to show the parents how he'd been teaching the basic skills to a bunch of relatively slow swimmers, this was bona fide water polo, and there was plenty of swift swimming and grabbin' and grapplin', as the coach liked to call it. No one kept score, and it was more fun than anything else. But the vast improvement in the skills of the team members was obvious to all.

While the young participants were getting showered and dressed, Sandy and the parents went to one of the YMCA's meeting rooms, where a mid-afternoon meal was being catered. "I have a surprise for you," he told them. "All the games at the Colorado tournament were video-taped by the host organization, and I have a copy of our matchup with the Missouri team. If you can sit for a few minutes, I'll breeze through it, and you can watch your kids in action in a regulation game contested in one of the fanciest indoor facilities in the country."

He'd picked the encounter with Missouri because the subs had played extensively after the starters had rung up a comfortable halftime lead, and thus the parents could watch *every* team member contributing to the triumph. He skipped along, jumping hastily from one score to another, narrating in the process, and as he did, the youngsters slowly entered the room fully-clothed and undoubtedly hungry. Most gathered with their parents in small groups.

Bringing the video to an end as the chatter increased, Sandy raised his voice and asked everyone to be seated in the chairs that were placed around the room. It took awhile, but eventually the various family members were all sitting and giving him their attention. "First, and always," he started, "I'd like to thank you moms and dads for your support. We've come a long way in the past 15 months, and you were the ones who made it possible. The YMCA also deserves recognition. It was the Y that brought me into swimming and water polo when I was younger, and it's the Y that pays me a salary for serving as Head Lifeguard and gives us pool time for practicing water polo. In case you didn't know, or have forgotten, it's the Y that's picking up the cost for us to use the larger and deeper college pool on Wednesday nights. Right now we're meeting in the Downtown YMCA building. There's more, but you get my point. This is a terrific organization that serves our community in dozens of different ways."

There was a shuffling of feet, but mostly the audience remained quiet as the Y coach continued. "I'd like to recognize two of our staff members, Tina and Lydia, and my assistant coach, Keith. They've helped me, and our team, on countless occasions. Please stand." The three individuals did as instructed and received a round of applause. "And I'd be remiss if I didn't also express my appreciation for my family members, who've welcomed me back home after I spent six years in California. Please stand." In a rear corner of the room, Sandy's dad, mom, sister, and grandparents all waved and were properly recognized.

"Now to our team members. Let me reintroduce each one to you." He had them line up along one wall as he called out their names, one by one. "Hector, Savannah, Ben, Nona, Jose, Princess, Warner, Wanda, Junior, Janis, Ellery, Delia, Clayton, Beatrice, Tommy, Cindy, Leland … and some of our newest team members who joined over the summer and autumn months … Jack and Jill, Alden, Missy, and Erin." He paused, caught his breath. "Every player is important. You know what I like to tell you. *At the Y, everyone plays.* But I've deliberately left one player to introduce until the very end. Please stand up, Lexie."

The entire room turned and watched as the tall young lady with the broad shoulders joined the others in the line. "Today is Lexie's birthday. She's turning 13." There were several quirky comments from the onlookers. "More than that, she received the Most Valuable Player Award from amongst all the girls on the six teams entered at the recent tournament in Colorado." The room burst into raucous applause, and Sandy said, trying to make himself heard, "THIS IS OUR TEAM!"

When the noise finally subsided, he spoke quickly. "It's time to eat, but before we do, I want to inform you that we have a new nickname. It was selected by the players themselves. We are now the YMCA Water Polo Stingrays." Shouts of joy emerged from the kids. "Now let's bow our heads and give thanks for the many blessings we've received, and then we can chow down."

* * * * *

Somewhere in the restaurant's kitchen, a platter was dropped, and because of the clatter, Sandy was unable to hear what Champ had said. He leaned across the table and asked, "Could you repeat that?"

The former YMCA Director of Aquatics and coach, now retired, had a broad grin on this face. "I said I believe that congratulations are in order."

"Thanks. The kids *did* perform well at the recent tournament in Colorado. We tied for second with a record of three wins, one tie, and one loss. The only team to beat us went out to California earlier in the year and won a big tourney there. Very impressive. Even more impressive, our girl Lexie received the Most Valuable Player

Award. Of all the girls in the competition, she was recognized as the best. The worst part of the trip was the weather ..."

"I'm not referring to the trip you took," the ol' coach interrupted. "I'm talking about you and Kristina becoming engaged." He reached across the table and took both of Kristina's hands in his own. "Sandy's told me all about you during our previous lunches. I'm happy to be meeting you in person. You're even more lovely than he indicated."

Blushing, Kristina replied, "He's told me a lot about you, too, Coach."

"Call me Champ. What're your plans for the future?"

"We're not going to get married for at least a year. Well, maybe not quite. We're aiming for next September. I've just earned my two-year Associates degree at our community college and will be moving forward toward a four-year degree in nursing. I'm still living at home and am lifeguarding at the Y. My only major expenses are for college tuition and the necessary books. So I hope to set some money aside." She let go of Champ's hands and reached out to grasp one of Sandy's. "He's quite a catch, don't you think?"

"Hmmm," Champ cast a discerning eye toward the large young man at the table. "I think he's getting the better part of the deal. So let's order, shall we?"

It was the usual for Champ and Sandy, a club sandwich and the salmon lunch special, respectively. Kristina surprised them both by ordering only dessert, a slice of key lime pie.

"How about you, Sandy?" asked Champ as the waiter delivered their orders. "What's ahead for you?"

"I've signed on for a second year as Head Lifeguard at the Y, and much to my surprise, I've been removed from the hourly payroll and given a salaried position that includes coaching the water polo kids. It means about $3,000 more per year than I've been receiving, plus there are a few other perks. I like the Y, always have since I first became involved as a youngster, and I'm thinking about making it my career."

Munching on his sandwich, Champ nodded. "Not everyone is cut out for a Y career. After I returned home from the Army, I thought I was going to become a journalist, and then I attended law school to expand my options. As I've told you previously,

Sandy, I had a chance to serve as an assistant editor for *Swimming World* magazine, but I didn't want to live in LA. I also found myself disliking law school. What to do? I'd been a long-time YMCA member ever since my teen days, and while attending college, I was teaching swimming at the local YMCA and coaching swimming at the nearby YWCA – one of the few men in those days willing to work with the ladies – and somehow everything fell into place for me. When I was offered a salaried position with the YMCA, much like you, Sandy, I decided to make it my career."

"How old were you, Champ?" Kristina wondered.

"Almost exactly Sandy's age … just a few months short of turning 26."

"I turned 26 the other day," Sandy said, "and Kristina almost didn't accept my proposal. She once told me that anyone over 25 was too old for her."

Kristina laughed. "That's what I said. But my parents convinced me that Sandy still has some potential despite being such an ol' timer."

It was Champ's turn to laugh. "I guess I'm the real ol' timer. I just turned 82. Have had some serious health problems lately but still swim for fitness when I can. I go to the Downtown YMCA to swim laps and socialize. Every now and then, I bring along a water polo ball and pass it around with a couple of my pool pals. But by the time Sandy's kids are working-out later in the day, I'm at home and awakening from my afternoon snooze." He winked at his young friends and then added, "I'm glad I decided against becoming an attorney, and I've never been a professional journalist, but I've done a lot of writing as a hobby. Looking back, I believe I did what I was called to do."

There was a pause in the conversation as all three concentrated on their food. Finally Sandy said, "It seems to me, Champ, that somehow you managed to combine a YMCA career with your love for water polo. How'd you do that?"

"I had help from my YMCA friends and from my water polo friends. No one succeeds alone. We all learn to depend on others for support. Also, I worked long hours … I put in extra time year after year … and I tried to mesh the Y's philosophy with my water polo coaching philosophy. As you know, the Y emphasizes the four values of caring, honesty, respect, and responsibility. As a coach, I translated these values into teamwork, team tactics, fair play, and good sportsmanship. Seemed appropriate then. Still does. I wanted to win, and I was disappointed, mostly for my athletes, whenever we lost. But it's the underlying values that count, that will be remembered long after the scores have been forgotten."

"You always give me good advice," Sandy said, "and I appreciate it."

The ol' coach leaned forward and looked first at Sandy and then at Kristina. "I have one more thing to tell you. Don't let *anything* get in the way of your love for each other. I learned how important this is at an early age from my parents. The religious foundation that my church involvement gave me over the years simply strengthened my belief that love is the bottom line. I wouldn't be what I am, where I am, who I am without my wife and daughter and two grandchildren. So as you two get ready to embark on a life together, I pass on my love to you."

* * * * *

Everything has changed, Sandy thought, as he sat on the long bench that ran the length of the lap pool in the Downtown YMCA Aquatic Center. Gosh, isn't that exactly what I told myself when I walked into this same pool after returning home from California? Then, as now, there were swimmers churning up and down in the one pool while a class was taking place in the adjacent warm-water therapy pool. The lifeguard on duty was the same one who'd approached him on that day which seemed so long ago, a pretty blonde who now smiled as he waved at her.

Some things have changed, he realized, while others haven't. This is the same Y where he'd learned to swim as a child and then practiced with the swim squad. Where he'd been introduced to water polo, leading to his departure for California to eventually become an All-American in the sport. Where he'd been a lifeguard himself. The Y's values remained the same, enabling the organization to continue serving as a force for good in the community.

His family unit remained the same. Oh, everyone was a bit older, but they still gathered around the dinner table most evenings, his parents and grandparents and sister. The church where he grew up was still standing on the corner, and he was attending services on Sunday mornings, as he'd done so often in the past. But now he was also teaching a Sunday School class. That was one change. What else?

Well, he was now the Head Lifeguard at the Y, on the staff as a salaried employee. He was engaged to be married to the most beautiful lifeguard in the world, who at that very moment was standing on the deck across from him and surveying the scene, making sure everyone was safe. As he looked at her, his smile broadened, and so did hers as she smiled back at him.

"Time to remove the lane ropes," he shouted across the pool. As he did so, the doors to the locker rooms swung open, and a flock of youngsters came charging into the pool area. Here they were, yet another change. The Y's water polo kids. They knew what to do. The oldest ones opened the aquatic equipment room and carried out the two goals and set them up at opposite ends of the pool. The younger ones grabbed the ball bag and all the caps and brought them to their coach. Some others, including Lexie, he saw, assisted Kristina in lifting out the lane ropes.

When someone had mentioned to Lexie at the recent Thanksgiving Weekend gathering of the team members and their parents that she was the star of the team, the Whiz as the local newspaper had called her, she had a ready retort. "I can't speak for the boys, but for the girls in our program, we're all in this together. We're all whizzes. In fact, we're the Misses of the Whizzes." It was an amusing and pretty good concept for a girl who'd just turned 13. Hopefully, Sandy murmured to himself, his young water poloists were being taught more than merely how to pass and catch and shoot a ball. They were learning about the importance of caring, honesty, respect, and responsibility.

"Okay," he shouted over the noise from the adjoining pool, "let's get going. We have a lot of work to do today."

From amidst the collection of boys and girls came the chorus of voices that now marked the beginning of all their practices and games and brought them together as a team. "Stingrays Forever!"

Author Chuck Hines with the engraved vase he received for being awarded the 2013 Paragon Prize from the International Swimming Hall of Fame in recognition of his 55 years of leadership in water polo. The Paragon is presented to just one person in the water polo world annually with recipients to date coming from Canada, Cuba, Europe, South America, and the United States.

AUTHOR'S AWARDS AND ACHIEVEMENTS

* Midwest AAU swimming champion, 1953.

* Military service with the U.S. Army, 1953-1955, including a one-year tour of duty in Korea. Received the Korean War Service medal.

* YMCA International Invitational Water Polo Championships, all-tournament team, 1959.

* YMCA All-America water polo player, 1962, 1963, 1966.

* Author, *Learning To Play Water Polo*, 1962.

* AAU Honorable Mention All-America water polo player, 1964.

* ASCA Water Polo Committee Chairman, 1964-1968.

* YMCA Water Polo Committee Chairman, 1965-1976.

* AAU Women's Water Polo Committee Chairman, 1965-1976.

* U.S. Olympic Water Polo Committee Member (and Secretary), 1965-1976.

* YMCA Senior Director Certificate, 1967.

* Author, *How to Play and Teach Water Polo*, 1967. Republished in London, England, 1969.

* Community Leader of America Award, 1969.

* YMCA Water Polo Coach of the Year, 1969.

* Southeast AAU Masters swimming champion, 1972-1981.

* Coach, Junior Olympic Water Polo Championships, gold medal team, 1972, and silver medal teams, 1971, 1973, 1975.

* ASCA Age Group Water Polo Coach of the Year, 1973.

* AAU Women's Water Polo Coach of the Year, 1975.

* Coach, World Women's Water Polo Club Championships, 1977.

* YMCA Distinguished Director of Physical Education Award, 1984.

* YMCA International Programming Recognition, 1992.

* Western North Carolina Sports Hall of Fame, 1994.

* Olympic Torchbearer, 1996.

* Gold medallion for Volunteerism, Summer Olympic Games, 1996.

* Western North Carolina Humanitarian Award, 1998.

* USWFA Top 100 Aquatic Leaders in the U.S., 2005.

* YMCA 20 Most Unforgettable Leaders Recognition, 2006.

* U.S. Pioneer Coaches of Women's Water Polo Hall of Honor, 2006.

* Author, *A Walk on the Y'ld Side,* 2007.

* Author, *Water Polo the Y's Way,* 2009. Republished in 2012.

* Founder and Chairman, U.S. Pioneer Players of Women's Water Polo Hall of Honor, 2009.

* Historian, American Water Polo, 2011-2014.

* International Swimming Hall of Fame Paragon Prize, 2013.

* USA Water Polo Legends of the Game Recognition, 2013.

* Author, *Water Polo Whiz,* 2014.

Made in the USA
San Bernardino, CA
19 December 2014